Don't Look Back

LOOK FOR THE OTHER BOOKS IN THIS
INSPIRATIONAL SERIES FROM BANTAM BOOKS.

clearwater crossing

Don't Look Back

laura peyton roberts

BANTAM BOOKS
NEW YORK • TORONTO • LONDON • SYDNEY • AUCKLAND

RL 5.8, age 12 and up
DON'T LOOK BACK
A Bantam Book/November 2001

ISBN 0-553-49379-5

Visit us on the Web! www.randomhouse.com/teens
Educators and librarians, for a variety of teaching tools, visit us at
www.randomhouse.com/teachers

Published simultaneously in the United States and Canada

Bantam Books is an imprint of Random House Children's Books, a
division of Random House, Inc. BANTAM BOOKS and the rooster
colophon are registered trademarks of Random House, Inc.
Bantam Books, 1540 Broadway, New York, New York 10036.

PRINTED IN THE UNITED STATES OF AMERICA

OPM   10   9   8   7   6   5   4   3   2   1

For Lindsay, Megan, and Renee,
one last time

The end of a matter is better than its beginning, and patience is better than pride.

Ecclesiastes 7:8

One

"I can't believe I'm finally sixteen!" Melanie Andrews told her boyfriend, Jesse Jones.

"You'd better be. This is one heck of a party if you're just faking," he said, his grin white against his summer tan. He was wearing Hawaiian-print swim trunks and nothing else, his brown hair falling in still-damp spikes over his blue eyes.

"Hey, Melanie!" Ben Pipkin cried from the diving board. "This one's for you!"

He launched his bony chest and baggy red shorts off the Andrewses' diving board, tucking his body into a cannonball that splashed down dangerously close to the edge of the rectangular swimming pool. A curved sheet of water jumped out of the pool, arced up over the edge of the deck, and landed across the two lounge chairs occupied by cheerleaders, one of them Nicole Brewster. The girls screamed indignantly, but some football players cheered, bringing a pleased smile to Ben's face as he swam quickly out of the area.

The big pool sparkled beneath the Missouri summer sun, and there were so many people in it that Melanie had lost count. Her sixteenth birthday party, originally envisioned as a small gathering with Eight Prime and a few other friends, had turned into a major CCHS event. Melanie's father had promised her a pool party months before, after she'd cracked her head open in a cheerleading stunt gone wrong, but even when she'd called in his offer, she hadn't expected anything so big. Peter Altmann, Jenna Conrad, Leah Rosenthal, and Miguel del Rios were all there, as well as Ben's new girlfriend, Bernie Carter. Nicole had brought her best friend, Courtney, her boyfriend, Noel, and her cousin Gail. Two other members of the new cheerleading squad had also shown up—Tanya Jeffries and Angela Maldonado—and so had five or six of Jesse's football teammates. As usual with parties in Clearwater Crossing, people had brought along friends who hadn't been strictly invited, but Melanie didn't mind.

The more the merrier, she thought, looking around at the crowd in her backyard. Her father was even part of the action—shaved, sober, and wearing a white chef's hat with his shorts, he was grilling hot dogs and hamburgers on the big built-in barbecue at one corner of the deck. Nearby, in the shade, coolers overflowed with soft drinks on ice, and the poolhouse was open too, with snacks and side dishes arranged on the bar.

"Melanie!" exclaimed Tanya, walking back into the yard through the gate nearest the driveway. She was wearing a bathing suit and flip-flops, a wide-brimmed hat pushed down over her black hair. "That's some car you got! I just went out to see it again."

Melanie smiled. "Thanks."

"Have you driven it yet?" Tanya asked.

"I wish! You know I don't have my license."

"No, but you got your permit last week."

"I just got the car today," Melanie reminded her. "And my dad doesn't want me learning on it. He hired a driving teacher, though, as part of my birthday present. I'm supposed to start lessons on Wednesday."

Tanya shook her head. "You are so spoiled! You didn't even have to take driver's ed with the rest of us poor slobs."

The fact was that Melanie had begged to take driver's ed, but her father wouldn't allow it. Melanie's mother had been killed in a car accident, and the idea of having his only child die the same way had turned Mr. Andrews completely against the idea of having his daughter drive. Melanie had started to think she was going to have to turn eighteen and move out of the house before she'd get her license, so she still couldn't get over the change of heart that had resulted in the appearance of a brand-new car in her driveway that Saturday morning. And what a car!

"Let's go see it again too," Jesse urged, nudging Melanie with his elbow.

"I'll bet you'd like to drive it," Tanya teased him.

"You *know* I would," he said, pulling Melanie toward the gate.

He didn't have to pull very hard. Melanie had been out to see her birthday present at least once every fifteen minutes since she'd discovered it. She couldn't help suspecting it was a mirage, something that would disappear if she so much as blinked the wrong way. To her relief, however, her enormous new car still squatted in the driveway, a bright blue bow on its hood. A trio of guys in swim trunks stood checking it out, their faces filled with envy.

"I can't believe he bought you a Hummer!" Jesse said for at least the fifth time, running over to peek at the car's interior through the driver's window. "This has got to be the coolest car ever made. Arnold Schwarzenegger has one of these!"

Melanie couldn't believe it either. For what her father had spent, he could have bought her a Porsche, but there was no way Mr. Andrews was going to put his precious daughter in something so small and crushable. The military-inspired Hummer was the closest thing to a tank a civilian could drive, and Mr. Andrews had convinced himself that Melanie would have to collide with one before she got hurt in it. High, wide, and already incredibly visible, the vehicle was also painted a brilliant canary yellow, just to add to the likelihood she'd be seen.

Melanie shook her head, a disbelieving smile on her lips. *I'll be seen, all right. There isn't another car like this in all of Clearwater Crossing. Maybe in all of Missouri.*

"We have to take this baby off-road," Jesse said, opening the driver's door and sliding longingly behind the wheel. "This thing will chew up the dirt."

"Oh, boy," Melanie said dryly. "That's exactly what I want, to get my new car all muddy and scratched."

"That's what these things are for!" he insisted. "You couldn't get it stuck if you tried!"

Jesse had offered to trade her his red BMW the moment he'd laid eyes on her Hummer, and for a second she'd been tempted. A cute, sporty car like that seemed much more in keeping with her image. But of course she couldn't trade away the car her father had given her, and the more she looked at it, the less she wanted to. Sure, it was huge, and intimidating, and not at all what she might have chosen herself—but it was definitely one of a kind.

The sound of another big splash from the backyard was followed by screams of laughter, making Melanie wonder if someone had lost their bathing suit.

"I'm going back to the party," she told Jesse. "Come find me when you can tear yourself away from my car."

"I'm coming," he said reluctantly, still looking back at the Hummer as they headed for the pool. "When did you say you're starting those driving lessons?"

"Not until Wednesday."

"Aw, man."

"Hey, Melanie! There you are," Leah greeted her near the poolhouse. "You missed Ben's big belly flop."

"It was bound to happen," Melanie said, shaking her head. "Did he lose his shorts this time?"

"No." Leah smiled. "Be thankful for small favors."

"So, sweet sixteen," Miguel teased. "Sweet sixteen and never been kissed."

"Yeah. Right." Melanie exchanged a knowing look with Jesse, and the love she saw in his blue eyes nearly took her breath away. "Sixteen, anyway," she said happily.

"Ooh, look," Jenna told Peter, pointing. The two of them had finally scored a lounge chair in the shade, and if they had to share it, at least they had a place to sit. "Here comes the birthday cake."

Mr. Andrews had just walked through the kitchen door onto the patio, a huge white sheet cake balanced in both hands. Candles sputtered on its top, their flames precarious in the summer breeze.

"Time to sing 'Happy Birthday,' " he announced, somehow making himself heard over the horsing around in the pool. "To Melanie and her friend Jenna, whose birthday was this week too."

Jenna sat up straighter, both surprised and pleased. With all the hoopla about Melanie's birthday, she certainly hadn't expected anyone to remember hers. Eight Prime had thrown her a little party at camp on Wednesday, with ice cream bars and homemade presents, and her family and Peter had made a big fuss later. Now she looked down at the silver bracelet Peter had given her, smiling as Melanie's raucous party guests slaughtered the birthday song.

"Happy birthday, dear Melanie-and-Jenna . . ."

"Happy birthday, you," Peter finished, whispering in her ear.

Mr. Andrews tilted the top of the sheet cake in Jenna's direction, and she could see her name in icing right under Melanie's. Getting off her chair, she hurried to join Melanie at the table where Mr. Andrews had just set the cake down amid paper plates and plastic forks. Melanie blew out the candles, and everybody cheered.

"You didn't have to do that!" Jenna told her friend, pointing to her own name. In addition to Melanie's sixteen smoking candles, there was an extra one off by itself—presumably to make up Jenna's seventeen. "It's your birthday."

"I wanted to," Melanie said. "Besides, now you have to help me cut the cake."

"I'd have helped you anyway." But Jenna couldn't deny she was touched by her friend's thoughtfulness.

They cut the cake into squares, transferring the pieces onto little plates and letting people pick them up from the table. When they had finished, Jenna took two squares back to share with Peter.

"Looks good," he said, digging in. "Mmm. It *is*. I wish Jason was here to get a piece."

Jenna just smiled to herself and took a bite of cake. For the past week, ever since Peter's family had decided to adopt Jason Fairchild, every conversation with Peter found a way of leading to Jason. Everyone in Eight Prime knew that the Altmanns had begun the lengthy adoption process and had applied to be Jason's foster parents in the meantime. There would be months of meetings, hearings, and paperwork before the Altmanns could be granted permanent custody of Jason, but they were hopeful that, as Jason's foster parents, they could move him into their home before the new school year started and Jason began second grade.

"Have you heard anything more about when Jason can move in?" Jenna asked.

Peter shook his head. "My parents had their fingerprints taken last week, and filled out background checks. They have to take classes to be foster parents, but it sounds like they can do most of those after Jason moves in. The social worker said someone is going to come and check our house to make sure it's safe for kids, but they haven't done it yet. Then there's something called a 'home study' for the adoption." His blond brows drew together. "The whole thing is really complicated."

"But you're still going to get him before school starts, right?"

"I hope so."

"Good," Jenna said happily. "Then he'll be moved in before the wedding, too."

She could barely believe that the wedding between her older sister, Caitlin, and Peter's big brother, David, was only two weeks away.

It seems like they just got engaged two days ago!

All of Jenna's sisters would be bridesmaids, but Jenna was going to be the maid of honor. Peter was David's best man. Every day seemed to bring some important new detail to be decided or discussed. The ceremony would be in the morning, at the

Conrads' church, followed by a luncheon reception at the Lakehouse Lodge. Trinity, the band Jenna had recently joined, was making its re-debut at the reception, and Jenna could barely even hear the word *wedding* lately without being overcome with excitement.

"Isn't that Nicole's boyfriend?" Peter asked abruptly, pointing with his fork. "Who's he talking to?"

Jenna looked toward the far end of the yard, where Noel was deep in discussion with a slender girl in a silver bikini. The girl tossed her chin-length black hair and sunlight glinted off its dyed red streaks.

"That's Nicole's cousin from Mapleton. Gail."

Peter's eyes narrowed a bit. "Is it my imagination . . . or are those two, well . . . flirting?"

Jenna's brows flew up. Now that Peter mentioned it, there was an awful lot of hair tossing going on. And Noel seemed to be laughing indiscriminately at everything Gail said.

"If that's Nicole's cousin, I'm sure it's nothing," Peter decided.

"I don't like how that looks at all," Jenna said at the exact same time.

They both turned their heads to look for Nicole. Jenna spotted her first, talking to Courtney near the open door to the poolhouse.

"I . . . I have this sudden irresistible urge for potato chips," Jenna announced, sliding off the edge of the lounge chair again. "I saw some in the poolhouse."

Peter wasn't fooled. "Say hi to Nicole for me."

"I'm not going to get involved!" Jenna promised quickly. "I only want to make sure she sees what's going on."

I should have just stayed home, thought Nicole, looking around Melanie's backyard party at all the happy, laughing people. Smoke still curled off the barbecue, but the hot activity now was a game of water volleyball that Miguel and Leah had started. The few people who hadn't wanted to play were lying around on lounge chairs, sunning, gossiping, and complaining about how full they were. Everyone seemed to be having a blast.

Everyone but her.

"Is something the matter?" Noel asked from the lounge chair next to hers.

"No," she snapped. "Why would there be?"

"How the hell would I know? You just seem awfully quiet."

"I'm tired, that's all. If you're so full of energy, why don't you go play volleyball?"

It looks like there's an open spot next to Gail, she felt like adding, but a sarcastic comment like that might have given him the impression she cared, which she didn't. She cared so little, in fact, that she didn't even want to admit she'd noticed.

"Maybe I will," he said, sitting up. Sunlight glinted off the tanning oil he'd smeared on his chest, and despite the hours they'd already spent at the party, his dark brown hair was still arranged in such perfectly waxed spikes she could barely believe he would contemplate getting it wet. Noel was, without a doubt, the vainest human being she'd ever met.

"Go ahead," she urged.

"I will," he repeated.

"Do it."

He left at last, easing himself into the shallow end, where he took a position in waist-deep water. When the time came to rotate, he waved everyone past him, staying at the minimum depth.

I should have known, Nicole thought disgustedly. *No way is he getting his hair wet.*

Not that she had a lot of room to point fingers in the vanity department. Admitting that hurt, but she knew it was true. Not only was her own hair as dry as when she'd arrived, she'd touched up her makeup twice. Worse, the ten pounds she'd gained over the summer had made her so insecure about wearing a bikini that she had ended up borrowing a sarong from her mother in an attempt to cover herself. Mrs. Brewster had been delighted by what she'd

12

misinterpreted as Nicole's newfound modesty and had told Nicole how cute she looked—a bad sign on any day.

I look like an old lady, Nicole thought unhappily, adjusting the sarong for the hundredth time. When she was lying down, her stomach looked flat enough to lower the top of the wrap to the edge of her bikini. But the second she sat up she had to hike it higher again. Either that or suck in her gut until she turned blue. *It would be easier to lose the weight than put myself through all this.*

Except that it wasn't easier. She'd been trying to lose the weight ever since she'd gained it, with zero success.

That's why you're in such a bad mood. Not because of Noel.

She didn't even like him enough to care if he flirted with Gail. Although she did wish Jenna hadn't noticed. If Noel was going to start embarrassing her in front of other people, what good was he?

And shouldn't my own cousin be more loyal?

Ever since Gail had started speaking to her again, she'd been a thorn in Nicole's side, making fun of her weight, her clothes, and the fact that her mother was expecting a baby at the end of October. She'd all but stolen Courtney's friendship, and she'd practically admitted she was interested in Noel.

Not that I care, Nicole reminded herself quickly. *She can have him, if she can get him. She can't get him.*

It seemed strange that now, when Nicole was totally secure in her relationship with Noel, it no longer meant a thing. She had finally figured out that he was only using her newfound status as a cheerleader to make himself more popular. Noel was planning to run for senior class president, and having a thin blond cheerleader on his arm could only help. That was it. That was all she was to him.

And Gail is even less. How can he get any use out of her when she doesn't even go to our school? There's no way he's going to dump me for her. No matter how hard she tries.

In retrospect, though, Nicole kind of missed the days when everyone had thought Gail was the queen of the goody-goodies.

"Hey, Nicole," Ben said, walking by hand in hand with Bernie. They were both dripping wet, having just climbed out of the pool. "You remember Bernie, right?"

Nicole gave them a weak smile. By now there probably wasn't a person at the party who didn't remember Bernie. Ben introduced her every five seconds. He was so obviously, hopelessly smitten . . . and so was Bernie. Nicole glanced from them to Miguel and Leah, hugging every time their team scored a point, to Jenna and Peter, talking and happy on their lounge chair in the shade. Melanie and Jesse were refereeing from the edge of the swimming pool, some part of his body in constant contact with hers. Even

Courtney was exchanging splashes with some new football player she'd met. Nicole felt like the only person there who wasn't in love.

But at least I have a boyfriend, she thought sarcastically, with another annoyed glance at Noel.

Part of her wanted to dump him. Then she looked down at her sarong and knew she never would. She'd spent her entire junior year trying to get a boyfriend, and Noel was her only success. Except for Guy Vaughn, sort of, but that couldn't have ended worse. If she got rid of Noel, she could spend all senior year without a boyfriend too. No one to take her to the Homecoming dance . . . again. No one to take her to the prom . . .

That's just not going to happen, Nicole promised herself. Maybe Noel was using her, but two could play that game. *I'll be going to Homecoming with the senior class president*.

A delighted shriek from the pool made Nicole look. Gail was ratcheting up her flirtation, splashing Noel to make him chase her. He seemed more than happy to oblige, weaving between the other players so recklessly that he was in danger of wrecking his perfect hair at last.

That is, if I don't kill him first.

Two

"What do you think of this?" Mrs. Rosenthal asked Leah, holding up a cable-knit pullover sweater. "It's cute, isn't it?"

"It's awfully heavy," Leah said doubtfully. "How often do you think it will be cold enough to wear something like that?"

Mrs. Rosenthal laughed. "You're asking me? You're the one who's been doing all that climate checking on the Internet."

"Well, it rains a lot at Stanford, but I don't think it gets that cold. Layers are good. And maybe a Gore-Tex rain jacket. That's probably the way to go."

Leah's mother put the sweater down. "Well, I think we've exhausted this store, then. Where do you want to go next?"

Leah checked her watch. Miguel had gone to morning mass with his mother and sister, but he would be home soon. As much as Leah was enjoying the unexpected opportunity to do some college shopping with her mother, she didn't want to miss spending even an hour of that Sunday with Miguel.

"You already bought me too much, Mom," she said. "In fact, I've probably got enough clothes now to get me through sophomore year too."

"What about that jacket, then? If you want Gore-Tex, I think we're talking about a trip to the sporting goods store." Mrs. Rosenthal led the way from the department store back into the mall's main courtyard and started heading for the exit. She walked all the way to the door, then stopped. "Do you need a good umbrella, Leah? Maybe one of those superlight, folding kinds? Because we should probably get that here."

"They'll have them at the sports place," Leah said quickly. If they didn't, she could live without one. The important thing was to hurry.

But in the car it soon became clear that her mother didn't share her sense of urgency. Mrs. Rosenthal decided to take the long way around, so that they could make some other, unspecified stop.

"I can't believe there are only two weeks of summer left!" she said as she drove. "What are we going to do without you?"

Leah tried to smile, but smiles were getting harder to find each time someone broached the subject of her leaving Clearwater Crossing. She never would have believed it a year ago, but she was starting to think Miguel was a genius for choosing Clearwater University instead of one of the "good" schools she'd been so obsessed with getting into. If Leah had chosen CU, she'd get to see her parents every day, whether she lived at home or not, because they were both professors there. She'd get to see Miguel every day too, and sometimes her friends from Eight Prime. The rest of Eight Prime was lucky, going back to CCHS together, but for Leah and Miguel there were only two too-short weeks of togetherness left. . . .

"I thought we'd stop here," Leah's mother said casually, pulling to the curb in front of the local computer store.

"Here? Are you buying a computer?"

"A laptop."

"Oh."

"For you!" Mrs. Rosenthal announced, obviously pleased with her surprise. "Your dad and I decided you should have a new one for school."

"Really? Fantastic!" The cast-off laptop Leah had been using all through high school was slow and hopelessly outdated, but she'd figured she could make it work another year. Now she wouldn't have to. Except . . .

"I don't know what I want, though," she protested. "I haven't read the computer magazines or anything. I don't even know what the choices are."

"That's what salespeople are for," Mrs. Rosenthal said breezily, motioning Leah out of the car. "We'll just find one we like and put her through the whole dog and pony show."

Leah's heart raced with excitement, but by the time they'd walked into the computer store, she was checking her watch again, torn. She really wanted a new computer, and she appreciated her parents' generosity in buying her one. But how could she get charged up about preparing for college when going meant leaving the love of her life?

"After this, we'll go to the sporting goods store and get the raincoat," Leah's mother promised, making a beeline for a salesperson.

"Thanks," Leah said sincerely.

She stripped off her watch and put it in her pocket, resolving not to look at it again until they got home. She didn't have much longer to spend with her mother, either, and she wanted to enjoy their time together. Taking a deep breath, Leah looked around the store, trying to make the necessary mood adjustment. Under different circumstances getting a new computer would be a major thrill; it wasn't her mother's fault if now the experience was bittersweet.

Even with the watch in her pocket, Leah could hear the seconds ticking away.

"I see Jenna!" Jason announced loudly, pointing to the front of the church.

He was still living with his foster mother, Mrs. Brown, but he was spending the entire day with the

19

Altmanns, from morning service to Sunday dinner. Luckily, the service hadn't started yet.

"Yep. She's in the choir," Peter whispered back as the singers filed into their places. "And that's Jenna's mother at the piano. She's the choir director."

Peter's mother and father were sitting on Jason's other side. Smiling, Mrs. Altmann held a finger to her lips. "Okay, Jason. Time to settle down and listen."

"Where's Jesse?" Jason asked loudly, twisting around in the pew to scan the faces behind him. "How come he isn't here?"

"This isn't his church," Peter whispered, not daring to look at his mother.

"Why not?"

"I don't know, Jason. People go to different churches. You really have to be quiet now."

The first hymn started. The Altmanns rose to sing, along with the rest of the congregation. Jason stood up too, to make carrying on his conversation with Peter easier.

"He came here before," he insisted, pulling on Peter's sleeve. "Why was he here before, then?"

Peter searched his memory and finally recalled that Jesse had attended services the morning of the Eight Prime charity pumpkin sale in the church's parking lot. Some of the Junior Explorers had come too, and Jason had attached himself to Jesse all morning.

"That was just a one-time thing, for the pumpkin sale," Peter explained in whispers. "I didn't know you were expecting him to be here."

He would never say so to Jason, but he was a little hurt to learn that, too. He wanted Jason and Jesse to stay friends, of course. But was he wrong to want Jason to like him better now? After all, they were going to be brothers.

Jason motioned for Peter to bend lower. "The last time I was here, I pretended like me and Jesse were brothers," he confided. "Now you and me will be brothers for real. Isn't that weird?"

"God works in mysterious ways," Peter agreed with a relieved smile. His mother tapped him on the shoulder. The hymn was halfway finished.

"I think it's good," said Jason. "I'll like being your brother. When am I moving in, Peter?"

Peter gave his parents an apologetic look, then pulled Jason back down to a seat in the pew, where they could whisper less obviously. He knew they ought to be singing, but he felt sure that, under the circumstances, God would overlook one hymn's worth of whispering. As far as his mother went . . . he'd have to explain it to her later.

"I don't know," he whispered to Jason. "Your social worker hasn't told us yet."

The request to move Jason into the Altmanns' care was supposedly making its way through the large and confusing maze of children's services, but

21

sometimes Peter wondered if anyone really knew what was happening. Jason's social worker, Valerie Horner, had responsibility for so many kids that it seemed like a full-time job simply to keep them straight. And now that Jason was going to be adopted, Ms. Horner was turning him over to a different social worker, one who specialized in adoption instead of foster care. The result was that neither of them was currently on the job, and Jason's paperwork was stuck in limbo somewhere between their offices. Lately, Peter had begun to consider a career in social work. More people were clearly needed in that field—especially people with new ideas.

"Why do we have to do what *she* says?" Jason asked. "Why can't I just move now?"

"Because we'd get in trouble, and that could ruin everything. We have to wait until they say it's okay."

"I'm tired of waiting!" Jason said sulkily. "I think they're just lying. They're not really going to let me live with you."

"No, they are. Soon," Peter reassured him, praying he was right. "We just have to be patient a little longer. And it's better if we still don't say anything in front of the other kids at camp, just in case something goes wrong."

Jason paled beneath his masses of freckles.

"Not that I think it will!" Peter added quickly, reaching out to ruffle the boy's white-blond hair. "I won't let it."

"Promise?" Jason whispered.

"Promise," said Peter.

They linked pinkies, the new favorite method of sealing a deal sweeping through Camp Clearwater, and Peter found as much significance in the gesture as Jason. He was committed. He knew his parents were committed. He'd fight to the death to keep Jason now.

The boy was already his brother.

Jesse punched the Joneses' garage-door opener and was walking through the coolness of the triple garage to his BMW when his stepsister, Brittany, burst in through the door behind him. Her straight blond hair fell past her bare shoulders, her thin figure loose-limbed and awkward in a gingham halter and denim shorts. She had entered a strange, coltish stage that summer—older than a child and not quite a teenager—but the most striking thing about her was still her eyes, large and brown, like melting chocolate.

When she saw Jesse still only halfway to his car, she put on her brakes abruptly, pretending nonchalance. "Where are you going?" she asked casually.

"To Melanie's. Why? What's the problem?"

Brittany's brown eyes widened innocently. "No problem."

"What do you want, then, Bee? I'm in a hurry."

"You have to talk to Mom for me," she said,

dropping the act to rush to his side. "Could you do it right now?"

"You want *me* to talk to Elsa? What about?" he asked suspiciously.

Jesse and his stepmother didn't exactly have a warm, fuzzy relationship, but ever since Jesse had come home from his trip to California, there seemed to be an unspoken truce between them. She was staying off his back, anyway, and he had no desire to mess that up.

"You have to get her to let me go to public school this fall," Brittany said desperately. "I can't go back to Sacred Heart."

"What?" Jesse leaned against his car, his keys dangling in one hand. "Why not?"

"You know I hate it there, Jesse! You *know* I want to go to CCHS."

"But you're only in eighth grade this year anyway. What's the big rush all of a sudden?"

"I'm sick of going to an all-girls school." Brittany's lips pursed as if she had tasted something sour. "And if I have to wear that horrid plaid jumper even one more day, I'll vomit! You have to help me, Jesse. She's talking about taking me uniform shopping tomorrow."

"The world will keep turning if you wear plaid," Jesse said, even more reluctant to talk to Elsa now. "I don't think I should get involved in this."

His stepmother and Brittany had been fighting

about the private Catholic school Brittany attended ever since the Joneses had moved to Missouri. None of them was Catholic, but Elsa had it in her head that Brittany would be better off in a private school, and the only ones in Clearwater Crossing were affiliated with churches. In the end, Sacred Heart had been Elsa's choice, both because of its larger size and the all-female nature of the student body—and while she sympathized about the uniforms, she considered unglamorous attire a minor concession for Brittany to make.

"But she'll listen to you!" Brittany pleaded. "You can tell her that CCHS is a really good school."

"CCHS, yeah. But I didn't go to junior high here, remember? I'm not even sure what it's called."

"Samuel Clemens Junior High School," Brittany said immediately, as if she'd been boning up for exactly that question. "That's Mark Twain's real name, you know. He was born in Missouri—in Hannibal, up north."

"And I'll bet you'd like to tell me all about it, but I have to go." He held up his wrist, showing her his watch. "Melanie's waiting."

"Please, please, *please*," Brittany begged, grabbing him by that arm and trying to dig her heels into the concrete garage slab. "Just . . . just tell her you think I'd really *like* Samuel Clemens, and that you've heard it's a good school."

"Who have I heard that from?"

"From me!"

Jesse struggled to free himself, but Brittany held on tight. "I honestly don't even know why you want to go there, Bee. Why start a new school this year and then do it all over again next year? Why not just stay where you are until it's time to start high school?"

"Because if I start a new school this year, I know I'll get to go to CCHS," she explained, her eyes wide and beseeching. "I just want out of Sacred Heart, Jesse. I want to have boys in my classes. I want to wear normal clothes. I want to be like everyone else! Can't you understand that?"

He could, actually. He had never understood why Elsa thought Brittany needed to be in an all-girls school, but he could definitely understand why his sister didn't want a high school experience devoid of dates, football, and proms. Academics were all well and good, but everyone knew that classes were just how high schools filled up time between the real events.

"I just . . . I don't know what makes you think she'll listen to me. She never has before."

"Well, she's sure not listening to me." Brittany was still pulling on his arm. "Please, Jesse? Could you at least try?"

Jesse sighed as he peeled Brittany's fingers from his skin one by one. It wasn't that he didn't *want* to help her. It was just that everything in his own life was going so smoothly. For once. Wouldn't he be crazy to rock the boat?

"Please?" Brittany begged.

Jesse sighed again, trying to avoid meeting her eyes. "I'll think about it," he said at last.

Three

The Junior Explorers' bus hit a pothole as it rolled back into the parking lot at Clearwater Crossing Park on Monday, jolting Counselor Ben both awake and nearly off his seat. All the campers were yelling and laughing, making the usual afternoon din. He couldn't believe he'd dozed off.

"You were sleeping," seven-year-old Elton Carter informed him from his seat on the other end of the bench.

"No. Just resting my eyes," Ben fibbed.

Elton made a face. "Resting your eyes and snoring, maybe."

"Is your sister coming to get you today?" Ben asked hopefully, changing the subject.

Elton snorted. "You wish."

He did, actually, and when he eventually spotted Bernie under a tree at the edge of the pavement, his heart swelled with excitement. She had been collecting Elton after camp a lot lately, and even though it helped her busy mother out, Ben was pretty sure she did it mostly to see him. It couldn't be easy for her, since Bernie wasn't old enough to drive and she and Elton usually had to walk home from the park. That day Ben had his mother's car waiting in the lot, though, so for once he'd be able to drive them.

The bus stopped and the campers ran out onto the pavement in the usual frenzy of screaming and pushing. Ben grabbed his backpack with one hand and Elton with the other, towing the boy through the crowd to Bernie.

"Hi!" he said. "I have a car today. I can drive you guys home."

"Really?" She smiled, showing small, even teeth. "That sounds a lot better than walking."

Ben led her proudly through the lot to his mother's car. Until recently he'd been afraid to have Bernie around his friends, or even to be seen in public with her, in case somebody clued her in to his reputation as a geek. Bernie was just going to start at CCHS in the fall, so—unlike the students already there—she had actually thought he was some sort of cool older guy. And he had thought she was the cutest, sweetest, smartest girl he had ever met.

He still did, although now he knew she'd had a rep just as bad as his at Samuel Clemens Junior High. They had confessed to each other a week ago, and now everything was out in the open between them. Ben didn't care who saw them now; he *wanted* people to see them together. Easing the car through the crowd, he honked and waved to the various members of Eight Prime, just to attract attention.

"There's Melanie," he told Bernie, waving. "That was some party Saturday, huh? I *told* you I'd take you to the cool parties." Actually, she'd told him that, but why split hairs?

"Really fun," Bernie agreed. "And Melanie's pool is incredible! The whole house is."

"I wanted to go!" Elton sulked in the backseat. "I don't know why you guys got to go swimming and I had to stay home."

"No little kids were there," Ben said in a slightly patronizing tone.

"It was a *high school* party," Bernie added.

Ben smiled at the way she stressed *high school*. It made him wonder if she realized she'd been the only freshman there. And she wasn't really even a freshman yet—not for another two weeks.

"So what?" said Elton, unimpressed. "I can swim as good as anyone."

That wasn't true, but Ben let it go, feeling magnanimous as he turned onto the tree-lined street bordering one edge of the park. The sun was out, the birds were singing, and he was driving with his girlfriend—his *girlfriend*! He could afford to be generous.

"Hey," he said impulsively. "Bernie, why don't you come to dinner at my house Saturday night? I'll get my mom to make her killer fried chicken, and you can see the new computer game my dad is working on."

"Really?" she said apprehensively. "Your parents won't mind?"

"Are you kidding? They'll love it. My mom's been bugging me to meet you for weeks."

"It's strange that I've never run into her at the clinic." Bernie's summer job was at the weight-loss clinic Mrs. Pipkin had recently joined.

"Yeah. Strange." Less strange when a person knew the extreme lengths Ben had gone to to keep them apart, afraid his mother would embarrass him, but he wasn't about to admit that now. Besides, those days of lying and scheming were over. He and Bernie were a solid couple now. Their relationship ought to be able to survive a couple hours with his parents. "What time should I pick you up?"

Bernie smiled. "You know fried chicken isn't on your mother's diet, right? Why don't you ask her to make something that she can eat too?"

"Right. Okay. Any special requests?"

"I don't care what we eat," she said shyly, "so long as I'm with you."

"Yeah. Me either."

In the backseat, Elton pretended to stick his finger down his throat, making gagging sounds as he rolled around on the upholstery. Ben didn't care. It would have taken a head-on collision to wipe the grin off his face.

"So what are you wearing on the first day of school?" Noel asked Nicole. He had picked her up earlier that Monday night and now they were sitting on opposite sides of a table in Burger City—not exactly her idea of a romantic date, but, once again, he hadn't asked. "Are you cheerleaders wearing your uniforms?"

"I don't know." Nicole glanced at her half-eaten hamburger and abruptly lost her appetite. Their uniforms hadn't even come in yet, and she was already having nightmares about not fitting into hers. The sweater would probably be okay, but she'd been measured for that skirt at her absolute thinnest. What if she couldn't close the waistband?

"Don't the cheerleaders *usually* wear their uniforms?"

"I guess so, Noel. It isn't my call."

Sandra, the coach, or Tanya, the captain, would make that decision and let the rest of the cheerleaders know. If Nicole, who had moved heaven and Earth to get onto the squad, didn't care, it was hard to understand why he did.

Except that she did understand. She could practically see the fantasy playing out inside his head, the one where he was strutting down the hall with a cheerleader on the first day of school. If he was going to be elected class president, he needed to raise his profile as early and as much as possible.

"Well, just don't wear jeans or anything grungy," he instructed, making Nicole wonder if he was thinking of the secondhand overalls she'd been living in lately. "If you guys don't wear your uniforms, you ought to wear a dress. Wear that new light green one."

"Mmm," she said, pushing a fry back and forth through a puddle of ketchup. When she had first started dating Noel, the fact that he cared about clothes had been a huge mark in his favor. That didn't mean she wanted to be his dress-up doll, though. She hated the way he bossed her around.

"I can pick you up at seven-thirty. I want to get there early and park in front, but we won't go in until later."

Noel had a cool black sports car. He wanted to park in front so everyone would see it; he wanted to go in late so everyone would see them. A few months before, she would have thought he had the perfect plan. Now the whole thing seemed so staged and fake it made her kind of sick.

"That's okay. My sister is a freshman this year, so Mom said I could have a car the whole first week."

"Tell her you don't want it! You want to be seen with some pathetic freshman when you could be riding to school with me?"

Nicole shrugged. "Someone has to drive her."

Noel leaned back in his chair, studying her. His jaw was still as square, his hazel eyes as sexy, his dark brown hair as cool as when she'd met him . . . but somehow his looks didn't melt her the way they used to. In fact, now that she knew how much time he spent on it, his hair even seemed a little ridiculous.

"Are you mad at me?" he asked abruptly.

"No," she said, not meeting his eyes.

"Then what's your problem? Are you PMS-ing or something?"

Her eyes snapped up to his then, glaring furiously. "Why? Because I don't want you running my life? Just back off a little, why don't you?"

Noel looked shocked. Nicole was pretty shocked herself.

"I know what this is about," he said slowly. "You're mad because I talked to your cousin at the party Saturday."

"Don't flatter yourself."

"No, that's it," he insisted. "You're mad because I paid attention to Gail."

"If you were so certain that would make me mad, then why did you do it?" she retorted.

"Ha! I knew it! You're jealous," Noel gloated. "Your cousin's hot and you can't take it."

Nicole pushed angrily to her feet, knocking over her soda. It splashed across the table, running off the edge onto Noel's perfectly pressed khakis.

"You know what?" she said. "If you think Gail's so

hot, why don't you drive *her* to school? It's in Mapleton, so you'll want to start *real* early."

"I didn't say I wanted to go out with her, I only said—"

"Go out with whoever you want," Nicole snapped. "But don't call me again. I am *so* finished with you!"

She spun around in the crowded restaurant, ignoring the stares from the other diners as she stalked out to the parking lot. Head held high, she looked around for her car, only to remember that Noel had driven her there. Without a moment's hesitation, she started walking down the road. There would be a pay phone at a gas station or a convenience store or someplace, and she'd call Courtney to come get her. Anything was better than going back into the restaurant and spending even five more seconds with Noel.

I can't believe I broke up with him, she thought, lengthening her stride on the off chance he might try to follow. *And I didn't even know I was going to! It's exactly like what happened with Guy Vaughn.*

She had dumped Guy on the spur of the moment too, on their way to a dance at his high school. They had argued about what she was wearing, and the next thing she knew she was telling him she never wanted to see him again.

There's something wrong with me. Tears rushed to her eyes and her chin came down a notch, but she forced her feet to keep moving. *How am I ever going to keep a boyfriend if I can't even control myself? Why can't I stay with anyone?*

She took a couple of deep, calming breaths.

Noel wasn't worth staying with, she decided. *All he cares about is my being a cheerleader and how I dress and whether or not I stay thin. And himself, of course. I don't have to put up with that just so I won't be alone. Don't I deserve better?*

You had better, she answered herself immediately. *His name was Guy Vaughn, and you were such an idiot that you didn't even appreciate him!*

Her steps finally slowed despite her resolve to get out of Noel's sight. She made an abrupt right turn down an alley, finding temporary cover behind a Dumpster. It was a huge relief to be finished with Noel, but suddenly she was full of other feelings that weren't nearly as pleasant.

Like guilt: If all Noel cared about was skinny cheerleaders, could she honestly say she was any better?

And disgust: She had truly thought she had cured herself of being so stupid and shallow.

And regret: If she had any sense at all, she'd have stayed with Guy instead of dumping him and hooking up with Noel.

It's just like Courtney says, she realized, wiping away more tears. *What goes around, comes around. The only thing that could make this more perfect would be if Noel had dumped me. Or if he goes after Gail . . .*

The thought brought a chill to her heart. Would he? *Would Gail?*

Nicole took another deep breath. There was nothing she could do about it now. Except to remind herself every day that she hadn't lost a thing.

Covering her face with her hands, she slumped down to the pavement and said a silent prayer: *Dear God, I honestly thought I knew better than this. I mean, I really believed I'd learned a few things. But here I am again, right back where I started.*

Why does growing up have to be so hard?

"I need to borrow your curling iron," Maggie Conrad announced, barging uninvited into the third-floor bedroom that Jenna shared with Caitlin. Caitlin was out with David that Monday night, and Jenna was sprawled across her bed, reading the latest bridal magazine.

She gave her younger sister a put-out look. "You're kidding me, right?"

Maggie had the curliest hair of all six Conrad sisters. Mary Beth had auburn curls too, but Maggie's were longer and nearly as tight as springs.

"I want to try this," she said, shoving her folded-back magazine over Jenna's. "Look. If you curl curly hair you make it less curly."

"That makes no sense whatsoever." Jenna tried to push Maggie's hand out of her way.

"It would if you looked! You're not even looking."

"I don't *want* to look, Maggie. I'm right in the middle of reading something. Just take the curling iron and go."

"You're not reading," Maggie scoffed. "You're only looking at the pictures."

"What I'm doing is none of your business. I don't come down to your and Allison's room and bother you."

"Maybe we wouldn't think it was bothering," Maggie retorted. "Maybe we'd think it was *visiting*."

Jenna sighed. If Maggie had a point, she wasn't going to admit it.

"Just look at the picture," Maggie insisted, sticking it back under Jenna's nose. "I'm thinking of wearing my hair this way for the wedding."

The model Maggie pointed to was wearing long smooth ringlets spiraling down past her shoulders.

"You'll look like Scarlett O'Hara."

Maggie rolled her eyes. "Good! She was pretty. Besides, don't you think this style will go good with a wreath?"

"For the last time!" said Jenna, losing patience. "You are *not* wearing a wreath. I asked Caitlin, and we're all carrying bouquets."

"I asked her if I can have a wreath *and* a bouquet."

"The flowers are already ordered!"

Which was kind of a sore point with Jenna, since she had really wanted to help Caitlin pick them out.

Her many attempts to help plan the wedding had caused a fight, though, and Jenna had had to promise to stay out of all future decisions. If Jenna had to, it was the least Maggie could do.

"Just . . . Caitlin wants what she wants, and we all have to respect that," Jenna said. "Stop bugging her about that stupid wreath."

"You're not the boss of me." Maggie stuck out her tongue.

"Yeah? Well, once Caitlin gets married and Mary Beth goes back to college, I'll be the oldest girl here. That means whenever Mom and Dad aren't home, I *will* be the boss of you!"

Maggie stared, horrified, as Jenna's words sank in.

Oh, wow, Jenna thought. *That's true!* Somehow, in all the excitement of the wedding, she hadn't realized that before.

And I'll have my own room, too.

For years she'd been agitating for a room of her own, but all she had managed to do was switch roommates, from Maggie to Caitlin. With Caitlin leaving, though . . .

Wow, she thought again.

Strangely, she wasn't as thrilled by the prospect as she would have been a year before. If she had never shared a room with Caitlin, she never would have gotten so close to her older sister. She was going to miss Caitlin now. A lot.

But since Cat was leaving anyway . . .

A room of my own. For senior year! And say-so over my sisters . . .

There was nothing bad about that.

A slow smile spread on Jenna's face.

Nothing bad at all.

Four

"Peter!" Jason screamed from way across the clearing. "Throw me the football!"

Peter smiled at the boy's optimism. Even assuming he could throw that far, and he couldn't, Jason didn't have a prayer of catching it. Instead, Peter broke into a trot, running back to rejoin his group. They were lined up on Camp Clearwater's makeshift field to play a game against Jesse's boys, and although not long before Jason had asked to be permanently assigned to Jesse's group, that week Peter had switched him back and no one had said a thing.

"Let me have it," Jason demanded, running up to wrest the ball from Peter. He was wearing the new striped T-shirt Mrs. Altmann had given him Sunday, along with jeans and the same dirty sneakers he'd been abusing all summer. "I'm going to kick it off."

"You are, are you?" Peter teased. "Think you can kick that far?"

The field was only about half of regulation

length, but even so, the counselors usually did the kicking. Most campers couldn't boot a football twenty feet.

"I can today," Jason said, his grin missing one front tooth. Snatching the ball, he ran back onto the field waving it over his head. "I'm kicking! I'm kicking!" he shouted triumphantly. "Everyone, get in position!"

The boys from both groups scrambled to take sides between the end zones as Peter joined Jesse on the sidelines.

"Okay, Jason! Kick it hard!" Jesse called, apparently forgetting he was coaching the wrong team. "You can do it, bud!"

Jason's kick went the predicted short distance in the air, but a lucky bounce sent it tumbling end over end toward Jesse's team.

"Get in there, you guys!" Jesse screamed, almost as an afterthought. "Someone run it back!"

Danny scooped up the ball and, with Blane out front to clear a path, ran most of the way back to the end zone before he got tagged down. Peter half expected Jason to throw a fit about the lack of defense, but instead the boy started gathering his teammates for the next play, yelling orders left and right.

"Come on, Peter!" he shouted. "Tell us what to do."

Peter scrambled to coach his team, wishing Miguel were there to help him that Tuesday instead of working at the hospital. If the kids had been playing tennis, Peter might have had some good tips, but he didn't much relish coaching football against a starter on the CCHS team.

It's just a game, he reminded himself. *And these kids can't pull off ten percent of what Jesse tells them anyway.*

Peter came up with a play, then hurried back to the sideline to watch.

"Jason's in a good mood," Jesse said, joining him again. "Ever since he found out you guys are trying to adopt him, he's been a whole new kid."

"Yeah," said Peter, smiling. Then a new thought suddenly occurred to him. "You . . . you're okay with that, right? I mean, I know you like him a lot, but—"

"What? Cut it out!" said Jesse, slapping Peter on the shoulder. "I'm as happy about it as he is."

"I got him! I tagged him!" Jason screamed, leaping around with his hands in the air. "Peter! Peter, did you see me? I was great. I was *great!*"

"Or maybe a *little* less," Jesse amended with a laugh.

"Are we late?" Melanie asked worriedly as Jesse steered his BMW down the Andrewses' private road after camp on Wednesday. Someone she didn't recognize was standing next to the Hummer, which still hadn't been moved from the driveway. "That must be my driving teacher. I hope she hasn't been waiting long!"

"Relax," said Jesse. "She's working for you, not the other way round."

Melanie leaned forward in the passenger seat, hurriedly gathering up her backpack, towel, and the shoes she had kicked off during the long ride home, barely able to believe that she was finally going to drive a car. Jesse pulled in behind the Hummer, and for the first time Melanie was able to see the small car parked on its other side. The body style was nondescript, the paint was oxidized blue, and a pop-up sign on its roof identified it as a student vehicle.

"How embarrassing!" Jesse said, catching sight of it at the same time. "You might as well be delivering pizza."

"It's only for a few hours," Melanie said, reaching for the door handle. "And once I get my license, I'll be allowed to drive my own car."

"Man. I can't wait," he said, casting another envious glance at the Hummer.

Melanie jumped out onto her driveway, stumbling over her long, damp towel. "Hi! You must be my driving instructor," she greeted the middle-aged woman beside her new car.

"You're late," the woman returned, looking up from the stainless-steel watch on her wrist and leveling a gray-eyed glare at Melanie. Her hair was gray as well, wound into a bun so tight a person could bounce a quarter off it. "I'm taking those three minutes out of your lesson."

"Um, okay. Sorry." Melanie dropped her things in the driveway and held out her hand to shake. "I'm Melanie."

"Obviously." The woman's hands remained at her sides. "Get in the practice car, Miss Andrews. On the driver's side."

"You can call me Melanie."

The woman cocked a gray brow. She was chunky, as large as a man, and masculinely dressed in pressed navy pants and a sharply creased blue shirt. "Get in the car, Miss Andrews."

Melanie threw a despairing glance over her shoulder at Jesse, who was still idling in the driveway. He shrugged, as nonplussed as she was.

"Unless your boyfriend is going to be brushing up his skills with us, he should leave now," said the teacher. "He's blocking us in."

Jesse immediately began backing out. "I'll call you," he mouthed before he turned the car around and drove off.

"I'll just, uh . . . I'll just take my stuff inside and tell my dad I'm here and—"

"By all means. Take a shower for all I care. Shampoo your hair and set it on rollers." The woman tapped her watch. "You're on the clock, Miss Andrews. Feel free to waste as much time as you like."

"I, uh . . . I guess Dad knows where I am." He was the one who had hired this drill sergeant, so he ought to. Tossing her backpack onto the porch, Melanie trailed her teacher meekly to the student car.

"You want me to sit in the driver's seat?" she asked nervously, just to be sure. "I mean, you know I've never driven, right? You're not expecting me to back out. Are you?"

The woman heaved an enormous sigh. "If I didn't know what I was doing, I wouldn't be the teacher, would I? If I didn't know what I was doing, would your father pay me the good money you're wasting right now?"

Melanie hurriedly let herself into the student car, sliding behind the sticky black wheel without another word. She didn't even know her new teacher's name, but by now she was afraid to ask. The woman was totally intimidating. Melanie buckled her seat belt, then remembered that her learner's permit was in her wallet on the porch. Did she dare say anything?

No, she decided. *If we get arrested, I'm blaming it all on her.*

"All right, then," said her teacher, settling in on the passenger side. "The first thing you'll notice about this car is that I have my own set of brakes." She gestured to a pedal on the floor in front of her. "Unfortunately, I don't have a steering wheel, so try not to hit anything."

Melanie took a deep breath, aghast at the mere idea. Were accidents something they should be joking about? *Was* her teacher joking? The straight set of the woman's thin lips made a sense of humor doubtful.

"Before we go anywhere," she continued, "we are going to rehearse the parts of the car. Over and over and over. Then, when you convince me you know them, *I'll* back the car out onto the road for you to practice driving."

She wasn't completely insane, then. That was a relief.

Melanie's instructor drilled her on all the parts of the car until she felt like she could find them in her sleep. Accelerator, brake, headlights, horn, parking brake, windshield wiper, brights . . . They even got out and looked under the hood, identifying the battery, the dipstick, and all the places fluids had to be added.

"We should do this on your car," the teacher said. "Now that you've had a look at this one, see if you can apply what you've learned to the Hummer."

Melanie didn't even know how to open the Hummer's hood, but the instructor figured it out. The woman stared at the engine, her arms crossed over her ample chest, until Melanie managed to identify all the same parts they had just gone over. At last she couldn't stand it anymore.

"I, uh . . . I know all the parts of the car now, but I still don't know your name," she joked awkwardly. "I don't know what to call you."

The woman rolled her eyes as if annoyed by such trivialities. "You can call me Smith."

"All right, Ms. Smith."

"Did I say 'Ms.'? Smith is just fine."

"All right . . . Smith."

Smith closed the hood on the Hummer with surprising tenderness, then strode abruptly to the student car, backed it onto the Andrewses' private road, shut off the engine, and got out.

"Are you going to stand up there all day?" she asked Melanie, pointing to her watch.

"Oh. Right." Melanie hurried to reclaim her place in the driver's seat while her teacher got in on the passenger side.

"You can start the ignition," said Smith. "Then put your foot on the accelerator and drive *slowly* down the road until I tell you to stop."

Like I was going to drag race, Melanie thought, her hand trembling as she turned the key. A first driving lesson was scary enough, but Smith was making it terrifying. The engine came to life and Melanie eased her foot over the accelerator, barely pressing down. The car rolled forward, creeping over the asphalt, but Melanie felt as exhilarated as if she were cruising the interstate. *I'm doing it! I'm driving!*

"Stop!" Smith shouted.

Melanie hit the brake so hard that both their heads jerked forward. "What is it?"

"What do you mean, what is it? Just checking your reaction time. All right, go."

Melanie tried to swallow the panicked lump in her throat. *I really have to talk to Dad about his taste in teachers*, she thought, remembering the art teacher they'd had to let go because of his more-than-professional interest in her. *At least this one's a woman.*

Melanie risked a sideways glance at Smith as she began to inch down the street again.

I think.

"So I'll see you tonight?" Leah asked, stopping her convertible in front of Miguel's new house after camp on Wednesday.

"No, come on in," he urged. "You won't believe how much we've gotten done the past few days."

Leah gladly set the parking brake and followed him up the driveway.

The outside of the del Rioses' white two-story house didn't look all that different from when Jesse and Miguel had painted it for the elderly previous owner. The front yard was in better shape, though. The trees and bushes were gradually retreating under constant pruning, and Miguel had coaxed a patch of relatively weed-free grass to grow out in the center. It would be a while before the grass filled in completely, but bare dirt was finally losing the battle.

Leah trailed Miguel up the porch steps and

through the front door, where the real transformation began. The interior was now as light and airy as it had once been dark and stuffy. All the old curtains had come down, letting light flood in through every window. The entry hall and living room walls wore fresh coats of pale peach paint—just enough color for a rosy glow—and the hardwood floors in those areas had been stripped, refinished, and buffed to a high shine. A faded runner of oriental carpet extended down the hallway, lending softness to the gleaming wood.

"Miguel! The floors look fantastic!"

"Do you like the rug?" he asked proudly. "My mom got that for almost nothing at a garage sale. It cost us more to clean it."

"It's great," she said sincerely. "It just seems to belong there, doesn't it?"

A sudden racket on the stairs turned out to be Rosa. Miguel's younger sister jumped off the bottom step and landed in the entry, her shiny black hair swinging.

"Leah! I thought that was you," she said excitedly. "Come up and see my bedroom!"

"Where's your mother?" Leah asked as she and Miguel followed Rosa upstairs.

"Still at work," Rosa reported. "But when she comes home, we're ordering pizza! You ought to stay and eat with us."

Leah grinned, knowing restaurant food was a rare

treat for the del Rioses, who were watching their money more carefully than ever now that they'd bought a house. Mrs. del Rios worked long hours at her department store sales job, and Miguel contributed as much as he could from his internship at the hospital. They made every penny count, using mostly hard work and ingenuity to fix up their new house.

"Look at the curtains my mom and I sewed!" Rosa said, throwing her bedroom door open. "Aren't they cute?"

The floors upstairs hadn't yet been refinished but were scrubbed to a dull cleanliness. Rosa's room had been painted white, the new shade contrasting starkly with the yellowed paint in the hall. On either side of her open window, long printed curtains fluttered in the breeze, lengthwise stripes on their white background dividing garlands of flowers in shades of pale pink, rose, and green.

"Really cute!" said Leah. "They definitely brighten up the room."

"We made them out of sheets. Look." Rosa pointed to her bed, where matching pillowcases had been converted into shams atop a mint green comforter. More sheet fabric draped a small table being used as a nightstand. "Everything goes together."

Leah turned to Miguel. "Do you have flowered curtains now too?" she teased, leaning up against him.

"Come downstairs," he offered with a playful glint in his eye. "I'll show you what I have."

"No, thank you," she said, giggling. "I would like to see the backyard, though. Any progress there?"

Miguel made a face. "That depends on what you call progress."

The two of them went down the stairs and out the back door. The bushes in back hadn't been tamed nearly as well as those in front. A clearing had been hacked out in the center of the yard, but Miguel's attempts to water the ground there had only resulted in mud. A muddy path led to a large tree near the fence, and for the first time Leah could see the trunk beneath its branches.

"Hey, that tree's new," she said. "At least being able to see it is."

Miguel smiled and took her by the hand. "Come look," he said, pulling her across the yard.

In the shade of the spreading branches, he pointed to a fresh white scar on the trunk. Two names were carved into the bark: MIGUEL + LEAH.

"Now we're immortal," he said. "So long as nobody cuts down this tree."

"Or it doesn't get hit by lightning." Leah tried to laugh, but her throat was suddenly tight and tears rushed to her eyes instead.

"What's the matter?" Miguel asked worriedly, taking her into his arms. "I thought you'd like it!"

"I do," she whimpered, crying against his shoulder. "Oh, Miguel, how am I ever going to leave you?"

"Hey! You're not exactly *leaving* me," he protested, pushing her back far enough to see her face. "You're just going to college."

"I don't even want to go anymore."

She hadn't expected to say that, but the moment it was out she knew it was true. Her arms tightened around him, and all the years of effort she'd put into getting into Stanford no longer mattered a bit. She soaked his shirt with tears, her sobs getting louder and louder.

Miguel rubbed her back, trying to calm her down, but his tenderness only made her more miserable. Everyone knew that long-distance relationships never worked. What was she throwing away?

"I'm not going!" she declared. "I'll go to CU instead. Or, if I can't get in this late, I'll take a semester off."

"What? Don't be ridiculous!"

"Ridiculous?" Leah repeated, wounded. "My wanting to stay with you is *ridiculous*?"

"It is when it means giving up everything you worked so hard for." He moved a wet strand of hair out of her face. "I'm not going anywhere, Leah. I'll be right here when you get back."

That's what you say now, she thought.

But she knew the statistics. She knew the odds against them. And she also knew how many girls would kill to take her place. . . .

"Come on, Leah," he coaxed, folding her back into his arms. "I'm not saying it'll be easy, but we'll get through this. They have computers in the CU library and I'll learn how to send e-mail. Plus you'll be home at Christmas. Right?"

She nodded, the lump in her throat so large now she couldn't even speak. Everything he said was true. She knew she had to go.

And Christmas seemed a million years away.

Five

"Hurry up, Belinda," Suki whined. "You're always the last one dressed for swimming, and that makes us last in the water."

"It's not a race," Nicole said automatically. "Everyone just put on your bathing suit and let's go."

Her campers were changing in the cabin, and Nicole was using the break to flip through a new beauty magazine. Not that the pictures were particularly thrilling her that Thursday; ever since she'd broken up with Noel, thrills were hard to come by. She didn't regret her decision. She just hadn't expected it to leave her feeling so . . . empty.

"Yeah. Let's go, Beluga," said Meri, using the heartless nickname the kids had given the fattest girl in camp. "What's the matter? Did you outgrow your bathing suit during lunch?"

"Hey!" said Nicole. "Leave Belinda alone."

"She's always so slow," Priscilla complained. "She's so fat she can hardly move."

"*Hey!*" Nicole repeated, indignant. "Is that any way to talk to another human being? Belinda has

55

feelings, you know. She's not just a, a . . . *thing* for you girls to make fun of. You should all be ashamed of yourselves."

The way everyone stared at her was so pronounced that Nicole gradually realized she was the one who ought to be most ashamed. She'd hushed the girls on a couple of other occasions, but she'd never taken Belinda's side before. Not really. The shocked expression on Belinda's face said that loudest of all.

I'm just like Noel, Nicole thought in horror. *I only like the cute kids, and the well-dressed kids, and the skinny kids with no problems. I'm a terrible counselor!*

And with only a week of camp left, she didn't have much time to change.

"Besides," Nicole told her group, belatedly trying to atone for the past, "Belinda's lost weight this summer. Haven't you, Belinda?"

The chubby little girl looked at her as if she had just grown a halo. "Eighteen pounds," she said proudly.

Meri snickered. "Only a hundred more to go."

"Okay, then," said Nicole. "Meri obviously wants to spend the afternoon sitting on the sand instead of swimming, so I'm just going to let her. Anyone want to keep her company?" She glanced around her dumbstruck group. "No? Then I suggest you all get your towels and get down to the lake."

The cabin emptied in a flash, a sulky, disbelieving

56

Meri in the rear. Nicole and Belinda were left alone, Belinda still only half tied into her bikini.

"You know, they make tops with elastic straps," Nicole said as she undid the knots Belinda had made. "You don't *have* to have this problem every time."

"I'm sorry, Nicole." Belinda's chin dropped to her chest, quivering as if she'd been slapped.

"I'm not mad at you. I'm just saying . . ." Nicole heaved a sigh. "Forget it. *I'm* sorry." She got the ties straightened out at last and made a bow on Belinda's back. "Okay, you're all set."

Belinda nodded and picked up her towel, heading for the door.

"Belinda, wait," Nicole said impulsively.

The heaviest camper turned around, but for once Nicole saw the girl's face instead of the roll of fat around her middle. Her lips were pursed apprehensively, but her eyes were full of hope. "Yeah?"

"I just wanted to say . . ." *What do I want to say?* ". . . that I'm glad I was your counselor this summer. And that I wish I had been nicer."

Belinda smiled. "You're nice, Nicole. You're *real* nice sometimes."

It wasn't true, but Nicole accepted the compliment gratefully.

"It's just that, well . . . my weight is kind of a sore point with me. And I think when I used to look at you, all I saw was myself. I didn't like how *I* looked . . .

and somehow I put those negative feelings on you. Do you understand what I'm saying?"

"I get it," Belinda said, nodding. "You thought you were too skinny before and it made you embarrassed. But don't worry, Nicole. You look real pretty now."

"What? No! I meant—" Nicole snapped her mouth shut abruptly, wondering why she was arguing. "You know what? Thanks, Belinda. I'm glad you think I look better."

Belinda smiled, so pleased she almost glowed. Nicole tossed one arm across the girl's shoulders, and the two of them walked to the lake.

Miguel was hurrying back to the nurses' lounge when the nursing supervisor, Howard, stopped him in the hall.

"What are you doing right now?" Howard asked. He was wearing scrubs and a stethoscope, his normally bristly crew cut in need of a trim.

"Now?" Miguel held up the picture books in his hands. "I was going to swap these for some new ones. We have a big demand for stories today."

Miguel had been hired at the hospital as part of a program that encouraged young people to choose a career in medicine. He assisted the nurses on the children's ward and was mentored by Dr. Wells, a pediatric surgeon. Most of the time, however, he simply read to the kids, played board games with them, or did whatever else he could to keep their spirits up. He enjoyed hanging out with the patients, but he couldn't wait until he started medical school and began learning how to really help them. Every hour he spent on the ward only intensified his desire to become a doctor.

"Lose the books," Howard said. "I've got something for you to do in the lab."

Miguel complied eagerly, ducking into the lounge only long enough to drop the books on a table. He hardly ever got to visit the lab, although once in a while Howard would let him watch a test, or ask him to help hold an especially unwilling patient long enough for someone to draw blood.

The lab on the children's ward was a small, sterile room lined with counters and cabinets. Anything complicated was tested in the main lab downstairs.

"We've got these urine samples to test for glucose," Howard said matter-of-factly, shutting the lab door behind them. Lined up on a tray on the counter were six half-full plastic specimen cups marked with identifying information. "You've watched me do this before, right?"

"Yep. You just dip those little strips into them and see what colors they turn."

"Right." Howard took a container of test strips out of a drawer and dipped one into the first cup. "Hmm," he said after a few seconds. "That's weird."

"What is?" asked Miguel, straining for a better look.

"Negative for glucose. I'm not sure I trust that reading."

Howard examined the date on the test strips, shrugged, then took out another one. Dipping it into the specimen, he timed the reaction against his watch, then shook his head. "There's something wrong with this batch of strips."

"How do you know? Maybe there's just no glucose in that sample."

Howard smiled, pleased. "I'm glad you asked. When there's sugar in urine, you can smell it. That's how the Greeks discovered diabetes in the first place. Here, take a whiff."

He held the cup out to Miguel, who kept his hands at his sides.

"Are you kidding me?" he asked suspiciously.

Howard circled the cup under his own nose and took a deep breath, then extended it to Miguel again. "You'll do a lot grosser things before you're a doctor."

Miguel reluctantly took the cup and raised it to his nose. He couldn't imagine what might be grosser than sniffing urine samples, but he didn't want to ask. He flared his nostrils as if smelling the specimen, holding his breath all the while.

"I see what you mean," he lied, hoping he sounded wise and experienced. He handed the cup back to Howard.

"I guess we'll just have to do this the old-fashioned

way. They didn't always have test strips, you know." Howard dipped a finger into the liquid, then popped it into his mouth. "This is sweet, all right. I'm going to say about one percent."

Miguel's stomach rose into his throat. He couldn't believe what he'd just seen. Couldn't a person get sick that way? Weren't there *laws*?

"You have to practice a lot before you get good at estimating a reading. I'm as accurate as any test strip," Howard bragged.

Miguel smiled weakly.

"Here. You try." Howard extended the cup again.

"Um . . . that's okay. Thanks anyway."

"What do you mean, thanks anyway?" Howard asked, offended. "This is a good opportunity for you. With six samples here, there's plenty to compare against."

He expects me to taste all six? The idea of trying even one was so revolting Miguel felt as if he might throw up.

"So let's go." Howard sloshed the cup in his direction. "I don't have all day."

"I just think . . . I don't really want to," Miguel admitted nervously.

Howard stared, outraged. "Fine. I didn't know you were so delicate. But if you're too good to learn from me, then by all means, go back to Storybookland. Shut the door behind you."

Miguel hesitated, torn. He and Howard had been

through a lot together, and he had immense respect for the man. Now he had obviously insulted him. Not to mention made him furious.

"No, I'll do it," Miguel said abruptly. The last thing he wanted was for Howard to think he was some sort of wuss. Besides, if the head nurse said it was okay, what could really go wrong? Quickly, before he could change his mind, Miguel dipped his finger into the cup and put it in his mouth.

At first he tried not to taste anything, but the flavor was strong and insistent. And familiar.

"Sweet?" Howard asked.

Miguel nodded. "It tastes like . . . like . . ." And then the light went on. "Like *apple juice*! Howard, you *jerk*! How *could* you?"

The jerk was already laughing, holding on to the counter to keep from falling over. "You totally bought it," he gasped. "Oh! You should have seen your face."

"That is not funny!" Miguel said angrily.

"Beg to differ," Howard got out between guffaws. "It's at least *twice* as funny as you trying to trick me into thinking I had some report due for the board of directors."

"Oh." Howard had sworn he would get Miguel back for that little practical joke, but so much time had passed that Miguel had forgotten all about it. "But my report hoax was just silly. Your joke was disgusting!"

"I warned you you were messing with fire. What

goes around, comes around." Howard's laughter had died down to chuckles, but the grin on his face was the broadest Miguel had ever seen. "Besides, hospital jokes lend themselves to disgusting. If you weren't such an amateur, you'd know that."

"Amateur?" Miguel echoed, trying to bluff. "You haven't even seen the first page of my book of tricks!"

"Same here," Howard said with a twinkle in his eye. Miguel had the feeling the nurse *wasn't* bluffing.

"Yeah? Well, that still wasn't funny," Miguel insisted. "What if I had tasted one of the real samples by accident?"

"You don't catch on too fast, do you? They're *all* watered-down apple juice. Man, you need me if you're going to get through med school. Those interns will eat you alive."

Miguel couldn't hold back his smile any longer. Inside he was already laughing, but he didn't want Howard to know that. "Do they play a lot of tricks at medical school?"

"Are you kidding me? They dissect dead people at medical school. If you don't laugh about something, you won't last."

Miguel nodded. It made sense. "Well, at least I won't fall for this one again."

"You can thank me later," Howard said, slapping him on the back. "Listen, I have to get back on the ward. Get rid of this juice for me, will you?"

"Aren't you scared I'll play a trick on *you* with it?"

Howard paused at the door, still grinning. "Aren't you scared I'll get you back?"

Safely alone at last, Miguel laughed out loud as he poured cup after cup of apple juice into the sink. The smell was unmistakable now; it seemed to fill the whole lab. Miguel rinsed down the sink and wiped both it and the counter with a handful of paper towels. Then he threw out the plastic specimen cups and put the tray away, making everything shipshape again. He liked working at the hospital.

I'm glad I won't be leaving this job in the fall.

He could only imagine what Leah must be going through, ripping up a lifetime's worth of roots to take off for California. He was going to miss her until it hurt, but at least he wouldn't be missing his mother and sister at the same time. At least he wouldn't be missing his home, his hometown, and the patients who needed him. He'd have to cut back his hospital hours, but he'd be able to keep his job. He'd be able to see the rest of Eight Prime. Except for Leah's absence, his life would go on pretty much unchanged.

Miguel smiled as he left the lab. Maybe going to CU wasn't the most heroic decision in the world, but he was satisfied with it. Leah had made the choice she'd thought was right for her.

He knew he'd made the right choice for him.

* * *

"So!" Brittany began out of the blue at dinner Thursday night. "Jesse and I were talking about what a good idea it is for me to transfer to Samuel Clemens Junior High this year."

"You were?" Elsa said suspiciously.

"We were?" Jesse echoed, nearly choking on his chicken.

Brittany laughed, a practiced little chuckle. "Yes, silly. Don't you remember?" Her brown eyes begged him to say he did. "You were telling me how great CCHS is, and how it might be easier for me to transfer now, so that I'll already know some people when I start."

Elsa was staring him down, her icy blue eyes the polar opposite of her daughter's.

"I, uh . . . I might have said something like that. I don't remember." Jesse stuffed a huge chunk of carrot into his mouth so that no one could expect him to continue the discussion.

"I never said you could go to CCHS," Elsa informed Brittany. "And I *certainly* don't want you in public school while you're still in junior high."

"But why not?" Brittany whined. "You said I would like Sacred Heart if I gave it a chance. I went there a year and a half—how long of a chance does it need? I want to go to regular school now. I want to be normal!"

Dr. Jones looked up from his plate as if about to enter the discussion, then abruptly returned to his dinner. He almost never interfered where Brittany was concerned. "After all," he liked to say, "she's Elsa's daughter." Unfortunately his philosophy didn't do a lot for family unity.

"You don't know how good you have it," Elsa told Brittany. "I only *wish* I'd gone to private school."

"But you're not the one who's going!"

Elsa's eyes narrowed dangerously.

"I've heard good things about Samuel Clemens," Jesse said, jumping in to avert the slaughter. "Nicole's sister, Heather, just graduated from there, and so did Maggie Conrad. They liked it, and it's supposed to have high test scores and all that."

On the other hand, Rosa del Rios went to Sacred Heart and loved it, but mentioning that obviously wasn't going to help Brittany's cause.

"It's not academics I'm worried about," Elsa said darkly. "What about discipline? What about violence? Public schools are dangerous."

But they're good enough for me, Jesse thought bitterly. Brittany was such a pampered little baby, it was a miracle Elsa hadn't spoiled her completely.

"Have you looked around this town lately?" he asked. "It's not like we're still living in L.A."

"He has a point," said Dr. Jones. "I don't think safety needs to be a factor in your decision."

Elsa turned to her husband, astounded by his unexpected intervention.

"Pleeeeese?" Brittany pleaded, trying to capitalize on the momentum. "Please, Mom? Let me go."

"You think I should take her out of Sacred Heart?" Elsa asked Dr. Jones.

"I didn't say that. I'm sure you have other reasons for wanting her to be there."

"That's right. I do," Elsa said defensively.

"But if it's not safety, and it's not academics . . ." Jesse shook his head. "I really hope it's not the uniforms."

"I *hate* those uniforms!" Brittany cried, right on cue. "You just want to keep me there because it's an all-girls school!"

That was the stupidest reason Jesse had heard yet, but the guarded expression on Elsa's face made him wonder if Brittany had hit the mark.

"You don't know what boys are like," Elsa said tightly. "How they treat girls, what they can do . . ."

Jesse wondered if that was some sort of reference to Brittany's missing father. He still didn't know that story, and he was starting to think he never would. All he knew for sure was that Elsa was awfully young to have a daughter Brittany's age.

"How am I ever supposed to find out when you've got me in protective custody at Catholic school?" Brittany retorted. "I'm not a moron, Mom. Maybe I know more than you think."

Elsa's eyes widened slightly and Jesse was certain

she was thinking the same thing he was: Was *that* a reference to Brittany's father? The one Brittany didn't know, had never even seen?

For a full minute nobody said anything. Then Elsa finally blinked.

"I'll think about it," she said grudgingly. "But I'm done talking about it right now."

Brittany flashed Jesse a thrilled, grateful smile. Jesse hesitated, then smiled in return. Brittany had her faults, but she was all right—once a guy got to know her.

Six

"I'm never going to get my license!" Melanie complained to Jesse during lunchtime at Camp Clearwater. All the groups were eating together on the benches that Friday, giving her a chance to vent about her driving instructor. And after her second lesson the day before, Melanie pretty much hated the woman.

"I'll grant you she doesn't seem like the world's easiest person to get along with," Jesse said between bites of sandwich. "But if you don't get your license, she's going to look like a lousy teacher."

"I don't think she cares! That woman lives to torment me. She ought to be guarding inmates."

"You're exaggerating," he said, picking up his soda.

"You know what happened yesterday? I was driving down Solitude—a nice, quiet street, right? All of a sudden these two dogs run out and start, um . . . ." Melanie glanced around at the nearby campers. ". . . getting *friendly*, if you know what I mean. Right in front of the car!"

69

Jesse laughed so abruptly that his Coke spewed all over the dirt. He obviously knew exactly what she meant.

"I stopped, but I didn't know what to do," she whined. "I mean, what's the procedure for *that*? Are you supposed to wait? Go around them? What?"

Jesse was laughing so hard that there was no hope of his answering. Ben wandered over, intrigued by the ruckus.

"It's not funny, Jesse!" Melanie stomped a foot, raising a small cloud of dust. "I don't know how you can laugh."

"I don't . . . know how . . . you can't," her boyfriend managed to choke out.

"And I asked her! I kept asking, 'What am I supposed to do?' But all she'd tell me is, 'What does it say in the driver's manual?' I can guarantee you that particular situation isn't covered in the manual!"

Jesse doubled over, his face turning brilliant red.

"What are you guys talking about?" Ben ventured.

"My monster of a driving instructor," Melanie said. "She's just evil."

"Ha!" Ben exclaimed. "I don't care how bad she is—she can't be worse than the woman I took my driving test from. She *wanted* me to fail, I swear. Sometimes I still have nightmares about trying to parallel park with her in the car."

"Smith used to be a driving examiner. Now she has her own business terrorizing private students."

"Did you . . ." Ben swallowed visibly. "Did you say . . . *Smith?*"

"Isn't that stupid? Like she doesn't even have a first name."

"You poor girl!" Ben moaned. "Smith was my driving examiner! She fails everyone!"

"See?" Melanie cried, turning back to Jesse.

Jesse had finally stopped laughing. "*You* passed," he reminded Ben.

Melanie caught the look Jesse gave her, as if to say she could easily duplicate any feat of Ben's. She wanted to believe him, but still . . .

He's not the one sitting next to Smith in that little car. He ought to try it once. Then we'd see how tough he is.

"Well . . . at least if she's an instructor now, she can't be your examiner, too," Ben offered. "That's something to be grateful for."

"At the rate we're going, she's never even going to let me *take* the test. I used to think it was only my father who didn't want me to drive. Now the entire universe is conspiring against me!"

"Your father's the one who hired Smith," said Jesse. "Maybe it's still only him."

Melanie felt the ground lurch under her feet. Could Jesse have a point?

Here goes nothing, Nicole thought nervously, stepping out of her mother's car. The cheerleaders were having an orientation meeting at school that Friday, and Nicole hadn't seen most of them since cheer-leading camp.

They're all going to see I've gained weight and make a big deal about it, she worried as she dragged her feet toward the CCHS gym. Tanya and Angela hadn't mentioned her weight gain at Melanie's pool party, but they were two of the nicest girls on the squad. *Just wait until Lou Anne sees. Or that witch Debbie Morris!*

The thought made her wish she were back at Camp Clearwater, where people were less critical. The other cheerleaders hadn't exactly welcomed her with open arms, and even though she'd made some headway during cheer camp, who knew how much ground she might have lost since then? Nicole adjusted a strap on her new sundress, hoped her carefully styled hair wasn't getting ruined in the breeze, and forced her feet to keep moving.

What if Sandra has the uniforms today? And what if mine doesn't fit? I'll be the laughingstock of the squad!

After everything she'd gone through to become a cheerleader, Nicole knew she ought to be *running* into the gym, but her insecurity was ruining everything.

If nothing else, you ought to be excited out of gratitude to Melanie, she lectured herself. *If she hadn't dropped her position to give you this shot, you'd still be the runner-up. For Pete's sake, hold your head up and try to remember how badly you wanted to be here.*

Inside the gym, Nicole was the last girl to join the meeting. Sandra shot a meaningful glance at the clock on the gym wall, but Nicole had slipped in just before the two o'clock start time—she'd made sure of that. Sandra was a great coach, but she had no tolerance for slackers.

"Hi, Nicole!" Kara Tibbs said in greeting. Kara and Nicole had been roommates at cheerleading camp. "Isn't this exciting? I can't believe the season is finally starting."

"Here's the schedule for next week," Tanya added, handing Nicole a sheet of paper. "We're practicing every day from now until school starts."

Every day? Nicole skimmed the schedule in her hand and realized she wouldn't be able to return to camp. The day before had been her last as a counselor and she hadn't even known it. Considering that she hadn't been all that psyched about Camp Clearwater in the first place, she was surprised by how sorry she felt.

"Everyone, sit down, please!" Sandra said loudly. She was wearing her usual lightweight jogging suit, ironed perfectly smooth except for razor-sharp creases in the pant legs. A red bow held her black ponytail off her neck. In one hand was the ever-present clipboard; the other gripped a pencil. "I want to get started now."

All ten girls rushed to take seats on the bleachers. Nicole ended up in the first row between Kara and

Angela, with Tanya and Lou Anne at the ends. Jamila, Maria, Debbie, Sidney, and Becca crowded in behind them.

"It's good to see you all here. I hope you had a nice summer," Sandra said, dispensing with the greetings before turning to the schedule. On top of long practices every day the following week, she had scheduled an hour-long practice for that very afternoon—despite the fact that no one had expected or dressed for it. "I had to, because on Thursday we're going downtown to pick up your uniforms, and trying them on will kill at *least* an hour."

An excited murmur ran through the squad at the mention of uniforms.

"I hope mine fits," Kara confided to Nicole. "I grew an inch this summer."

Nicole only wished that up was the direction she'd grown in. She held her breath in panic, waiting for someone to take the obvious shot.

"It's dumb to measure for those things so far in advance," said Jamila. "I don't think I'm the same size either."

Really? Nicole twisted around on the bench to look.

It suddenly dawned on her that none of the girls looked exactly the same as she had at cheerleading camp. Some had longer hair, some shorter. End-of-summer tans and new styles of makeup seemed to change their features. Nicole couldn't be certain, but they probably didn't all weigh exactly the same, either. Kara looked thinner, and Tanya's arms seemed twice as buff. Debbie, conspicuously silent, might even have been in the same boat as Nicole.

"If there aren't any questions, let's go outside and work on our chants," said Sandra. "Football practice doesn't start until Monday, so we ought to have the field to ourselves. I have to make a quick phone call, but go on out and start stretching."

Nicole walked outside with the rest of the girls, feeling slightly more confident. Maybe her weight gain wasn't as noticeable as she'd thought . . . or maybe the other cheerleaders liked her more than she'd dared to hope.

"Your top is cute," she told Maria, testing the water.

"Thanks," Maria replied. "Cute dress."

Nicole's self-esteem climbed another notch. After all, she'd had these girls eating out of her hands at cheerleading camp. If they weren't all best friends, at the very least they were squad mates. They *had* to stick together.

Despite Sandra's prediction, football was being played on the field, although it obviously wasn't an organized practice. Eight or ten guys were running around with some balls, passing them back and forth and boasting about all the plays they'd make when the season actually started. Nicole recognized a couple of them from hanging around with Jesse, but she didn't know their names.

"That one in the blue shorts is cute," said Debbie, flashing a smile in the boy's direction. He must have noticed, because he and a buddy broke off from the group and trotted over to join the girls. Blue Shorts stood tossing a ball up and down in one hand, showing off his coordination.

"You girls practicing today?" he asked.

Debbie shrugged. "Just some chants."

"How about you, Nicole?" he asked, grinning charmingly.

"Me? Well, I . . ." She hadn't even known he knew her name.

"Chants," Tanya answered for her. "Amazingly enough, we're *all* doing chants."

Blue Shorts laughed.

I don't know his *name*, Nicole realized.

"I meant what are you doing in general?" he covered, speaking directly to Nicole. "Like this weekend, maybe?"

"Nothing that would interest you."

She had meant to be simply factual, but squeals of laughter from the other girls alerted her to the rudeness of her remark. The guy's face fell. The ball stuck to his hand.

"I mean, I'm going to a wedding," she amended quickly. "Guys don't usually find weddings too interesting, do they?"

"I guess not," Blue Shorts agreed, latching on to the opportunity to save face. He was cute when he smiled—dimples and good white teeth. "Too much yakking and not enough action."

His friend snickered, grabbed the ball, and ran back to the other guys.

"I guess I'll just have to wait and see you at school, then," Blue Shorts added flirtatiously.

"Um, yeah. I guess so."

He ran off as well, leaving Nicole amazed and the rest of the girls teasing her.

"Ooh, Nicole!" Kara giggled. "I think someone likes you."

"Noel's not going to be too happy about that!" said Maria.

Nicole tossed her hair. "I broke up with Noel."

"What?" Becca exclaimed disbelievingly. "Why?"

"He was getting on my nerves." Which was true, even if it wasn't the whole story.

Debbie gave Nicole an appraising look, as if she might have underestimated her.

"Seems Mark wouldn't mind taking his place," Angela observed.

Mark, thought Nicole. *That's Blue Shorts's name.*

Not that she planned to do anything about it. There was a time when she would have leapt at attention from a guy like Mark. But she was sadder and, she hoped, wiser now. If she didn't even know the guy's name, what did he know about her? That she was a cheerleader? She'd already been down that road once, and she hadn't liked where it led.

No thanks. The next time I get interested in a guy, he's going to like me for me.

"I'm thinking of trying to identify rocks with my group on next week's nature hike," Melanie told Leah. The two of them were tanning by the lake that Friday afternoon, not needed for lifeguard duty. They could hear the campers shouting and splashing, but their backs were to the water and the action seemed far away. "Didn't you do that with your girls?"

Leah smiled, remembering. In addition to learning some common rock names, she had studied for hours to deliver a big scientific lecture on the formation of the universe. Her group had unwittingly stopped her after one sentence.

"Yep. I'll lend you my rock ID guides if you want, but do yourself a favor and don't ask the kids how the Earth got here."

"What? Why not?"

"I had this whole big speech planned about the Big Bang and the nebular hypothesis, and I opened with this rhetorical question asking if anyone knew how the Earth got here. The next thing I know, Joy says, 'God put it here,' and my entire group agrees with her."

Melanie burst out laughing, sunlight glinting off her blond hair. "So what did you say?"

"I ended up dropping the whole subject and moving straight to the rocks. *I'm* not going to tell a bunch of seven-year-olds what God did and didn't do. Heck, for all I know, Joy's right."

"Do you think so?" Melanie asked seriously.

At the beginning of the school year, when Eight Prime had first formed, Melanie had been its only atheist. The varying degrees of religion practiced by most of the rest of the group had made her openly uncomfortable. Over time, however, Leah had noticed a change. Melanie seemed a lot more open-minded about God now than she had in September.

"I'm not going to rule it out," Leah said. "At least not until someone can prove otherwise."

"Wouldn't that be great?" There was a wistful expression in Melanie's green eyes. Her full lips twisted a bit. "Wouldn't you love it if someone could prove the existence of God one way or the other? I mean, either he exists or he doesn't, but whichever it is, we'd all know for sure. Wouldn't that be great?"

"It wouldn't be so great if he didn't. I like at least thinking he might."

"Yeah. But if it's not true, why believe it? I mean, don't you just want to know the truth? Whatever it is?"

Leah flipped over on her towel. "You know what I've been thinking about lately?" she confided. "I've been treating God like a scientific theory."

"How so?" Melanie asked.

"Well, science believes in things it can't see, if the invisible explains the visible."

Melanie gave her a baffled look.

"You have givens, right?" Leah explained. "Things you can see, or touch, or measure. What scientists do is make up a hypothesis that explains the givens. You can't see the hypothesis. You can't even prove it, except by the information you started out with."

"I think I'm with you," Melanie said slowly.

"Well, if you accept that God exists—this intelligent, creative, powerful being—that explains a lot of givens. Not only that, but it gives humans a reason for being here, some sort of purpose to life. If people have backcalculated his existence, that doesn't mean it isn't so. Scientists do that all the time."

A wondering smile curved Melanie's lips. "I get it."

"I heard this song on the radio," Leah went on, encouraged, "by a group called DC Talk, and one line jumped out at me. It went something like, 'I've never seen the wind, but I've seen the effects of the wind.' And I said 'Yes!' That's exactly what I'm talking about."

"Let them hear who have ears, see who have eyes . . . ," Melanie said slowly, feeling out the words.

"You're quoting the Bible now?" Leah asked, surprised.

Melanie colored slightly. "I don't think I got it right, but Peter lent me a copy I've been trying to read it. You know, just to see what it says. Parts of it make sense, but other parts . . . If you can believe it, I'm thinking of taking a Bible class at his church this fall."

"Really?" Leah tried to focus on the unexpected information, but suddenly her thoughts were running together like sidewalk chalk in the rain. The entire discussion had been ruined for her by that one terrible word: *fall*.

Who knows what I'll be doing this fall? she thought, sinking into depression. *The only thing I know for sure is, I won't be doing it here.*

Seven

"That's the best that song's ever sounded!" Jenna said excitedly.

She was practicing with Trinity in Guy Vaughn's garage that Saturday, and the band had just finished "Now and Always," the song she'd written for Caitlin's wedding. With the reception only a week away, the entire band was excited about their first gig, and every time they nailed a song, their enthusiasm grew.

"We're basically ready," Guy said. "We're hitting everything today."

Paul twirled a drumstick. "We still ought to practice one more time. How about on Tuesday?"

Evan was already putting away his bass, in a hurry to go somewhere else. "Can't on Tuesday. Make it Wednesday."

They agreed to get together for a final practice Wednesday, and Evan and Paul drove off, leaving Jenna alone with Guy.

"I guess I'll be going too," she said. "My mom

probably wants her station wagon back by now. There are tons of last-minute things to do for the wedding."

"About the wedding . . . ," Guy said, fooling around with one of his guitar strings. "I've kind of been meaning to ask you . . . Is Nicole Brewster going to be there?"

Jenna's brows rose on their own. Guy hadn't mentioned Nicole once since that awkward discussion they'd had about her when Jenna had first joined his band. So why was he asking now?

"Yes," she finally answered. "She'll be at the reception, anyway. I talked Cat into inviting all of Eight Prime. Ben's even bringing his new girlfriend."

Guy looked surprised. "Isn't it kind of expensive, inviting all those extra people?"

"They're not extra, they're our friends! Between our fund-raisers and Camp Clearwater, Caitlin and David both know them all. Besides," she added, playing the card that had convinced her mother, "the Lakehouse Lodge has a seventy-five-guest minimum for the room we're using. If we're paying for that many people, we might as well bring them, right?"

Jenna mostly wanted her friends to come because it would make things more fun for her and Peter, but of course she couldn't admit that.

"I guess." Guy started tweaking a second guitar string.

Jenna hesitated, torn between leaving and pursuing the conversation. It just seemed so strange that Guy would mention Nicole now, after all this time. . . .

Is it possible he's still interested? When Jenna had joined the band, he had sworn he wasn't—but what else was he going to say about someone he wasn't seeing anymore?

Is Nicole? After all, now that she'd broken up with Noel, she was free again. Jenna hadn't especially liked Noel. She couldn't quite put her finger on it, but there was something phony about him. Guy, on the other hand . . .

She was a fool to let Guy go.

Could the wedding be Nicole's chance to get him back?

Maybe I could be their matchmaker!

Excited, Jenna imagined ways of bringing Guy and Nicole together again. Maybe she could involve them both in a conversation and then wander off into the crowd, leaving the two of them alone. Or perhaps something more spectacular, like rigging a dedication so that they'd have to dance with each other . . .

That could be a little tricky, with Guy playing in the band. But if I did it during one of the breaks, when we're playing CDs . . .

Her heart was already racing with the thrill. She was positive that if she put her mind to it, she could pull off something clever.

Whoops, wait a minute, she thought suddenly. *What if he's asking because he was hoping not to see Nicole?*

Any scheme Jenna came up with in that case was sure to end in disaster.

She tried to read his features, but Guy was still fiddling with his guitar, his eyes not meeting hers. She had no way of knowing what was in his head, let alone his heart.

I'd better leave it alone, she thought reluctantly. *It's really none of my business anyway.*

The good stuff never was. All Jenna ever wanted was to help, but she'd had enough of her "helpful" plans backfire to realize that good intentions don't count for much in a crisis.

If I get in the middle of this, I could end up with both of them hating me.

Unless I can make it look like I wasn't even involved . . .

She considered that angle a moment before past experience carried the day.

"I'll see you Wednesday, then," she told Guy, walking away.

They'll just have to deal with each other on their own, and whatever happens, happens.

"Where do you think I should hang this?" Mrs. Altmann asked Peter, holding up a new framed print of a boy with a fishing rod lying on a grassy bank. "Do you think Jason will like it?"

"I like it. If he doesn't, you can hang it in my room."

"How about here?" Mrs. Altmann held the picture against the end wall of David's room. "Or would over the bed be better?"

Peter shook his head. "No, that's good. Just . . . maybe a little to the right." He was marking a spot for the nail when his father returned from the garage, a hammer in one hand and a battered wooden sled dangling from the other.

"Look what I found!" Mr. Altmann said excitedly. "Remember this?"

"Of course!" Peter exclaimed. "Where did you find it? I thought it was gone."

"Up in the rafters," Mr. Altmann replied, clearly pleased with himself. "I thought maybe we could hang it in here. For a decoration."

"That dirty old thing?" Peter's mother objected.

"Relax. I'll clean it up." Mr. Altmann winked at his wife. "If you're nice, I may even give it a new coat of varnish."

Mrs. Altmann smiled, her expression speaking for them all. Jason's social worker had telephoned late Friday afternoon to say that most of the paperwork had cleared for the Altmanns to become Jason's new foster family. If all went well, she expected to get the remaining loose ends tied up by Wednesday morning. Jason could potentially move in as early as Wednesday afternoon.

"Hey, what's going on in here?" David's cheerful voice asked, surprising everyone. Peter turned to see his brother lounging in the doorway. "My body's not even cold yet and you're already redecorating my room?"

"David!" Mrs. Altmann exclaimed a little guiltily. "I thought you were spending the day with Caitlin."

"Oh, I get it," he teased. "You didn't think I'd catch you."

"I'm so sorry. We were just—"

"I'm kidding!" David said, laughing. "Decorate away. In fact, tell me what you need done and I'll help." He strode into the room, a taller, blonder version of Peter. "Do you want me to move out the rest of my stuff?"

He had already emptied the room of everything but the clothes he'd be wearing in the final week before the wedding. After that he was off on his honeymoon, and then he and Caitlin were moving to Chicago, where David had landed a job.

"Don't be silly," Mrs. Altmann told him. "This is your room for as long as you need it. If Jason really gets here on Wednesday, he can use a sleeping bag in Peter's room until you leave."

"I don't mind sleeping in the den," David said. "That sofa is comfortable."

"Or I'll sleep on the sofa, and you can have my room," Peter offered.

Mr. Altmann smiled. "I'm sure we'll work something out."

"So what have we got besides pictures?" David asked, eyeing the overflowing shopping bags lined up against one wall. "Somebody's been busy."

Mrs. Altmann blushed but didn't try to hide her excitement. "Want to see?"

She began dumping her purchases on David's bed, describing each item as she went. "A few pairs of jeans, and some new shirts for school. And isn't this jacket darling? Mrs. Brown says he has a lot of clothes, but he's worn some things out and outgrown others over the summer. We'll have to go through his wardrobe when he gets here and see what else he needs."

She set the clothes to one side and emptied the next bag. "A backpack for school and a new pair of sneakers. I hope they fit."

"He can definitely use the sneakers," Peter said. "He's totally trashed the ones he's been wearing to camp."

The third bag held school supplies: a notebook, paper, pencils, pens, glue sticks, scissors, a hole punch, folders, dividers, tape, crayons, construction paper, colored pencils, a box of watercolors, a ruler, and a pencil cup.

Mr. Altmann laughed. "Do you think you got enough stuff, Helen? It looks like we're opening a stationery store."

"These things aren't very expensive, and it's fun to have all nice new supplies for school. I want Jason to like school this year and, hopefully, to do a little better."

Peter nodded reflectively, thinking his mom might be on to something.

"What's in the last bag?" David asked.

"A new comforter for the bed." Mrs. Altmann dumped it out and held it up for them to see. Balls from every imaginable sport bounced across a blue background. "Do you think he'll like it? Or is it too much?"

"No way. He's going to love that," Peter predicted. "You're about to have a total little jock on your hands."

Mrs. Altmann smiled. "I can't wait."

"Me either," Peter admitted.

"Me either," said Mr. Altmann.

"Me either!" said David. "And I'm not even going to be here!"

Then somehow they all started hugging each other, overcome by the joy of the moment.

"Thank you," Peter whispered to his mother.

"No. Thank *you*," she whispered back.

* * *

"They're a little weird, but they're basically nice people," Ben told Bernie as they walked to his front door Saturday night. "I know they're going to like you."

Bernie smiled reassuringly. She was wearing a blue gauze dress with the typical assortment of beads around her wrists and ankles. Rhinestones glittered in her short brown hair. "I'm sure I'll like them, too."

I hope so, Ben thought nervously. *Or, if that's too much to ask, I hope that at least you're not totally freaked out.*

When he had invited Bernie to dinner at his house, it had seemed like a good idea. She was sure to run into his mother eventually anyway, and her interest in computers *might* allow her to appreciate his father's programming genius while ignoring his fashion sense. Now Ben was wishing he'd never proposed such a crazy plan. What if the night was a disaster? He and Bernie had confessed what nerds they were, but when it came to his family, well . . . his parents took *nerd* to a whole new level. Ben really hoped his mother wouldn't treat him like he was five and make her usual embarrassing comments. And as for his absent-minded father . . .

I'll call it a good day if he's just wearing a full set of clothes.

Ben opened his front door and waved Bernie into the entryway.

"Mmm. Something smells good," she said.

The sharp, tangy aroma of barbecue sauce filled the house, making Ben's mouth water. "That *does* smell good," he agreed, relaxing slightly.

"Benny? Is that you?" his mom's voice called from the kitchen.

Ben cringed. "I've begged her not to call me that," he told Bernie, "but it's a totally lost cause. My dad's name is Ben too, and she insists that she can't call us both the same thing. I'd gladly go by Benjamin, but . . ." He heaved a sigh. "Parents. What are you going to do?"

"Benny!" His mother emerged into the entryway, a dish towel in one hand. She was wearing a flowered housedress the size of a shed, but she had fixed her hair and makeup. "I thought I heard you come in. And this must be Bernie!"

"Hi," Bernie said shyly.

"Nice to meet you, dear."

Ben winced a bit at the "dear," but at least she hadn't called Bernie his "little friend," the way she usually did.

"You look familiar," Bernie said. "I must have seen you at the clinic and just not realized who you were."

Mrs. Pipkin beamed. "Could be. I'm there every week. I've already lost sixteen pounds."

Ben held his breath, wondering how Bernie

would reply. Since she entered data for all the clients at the clinic, she knew exactly what his mother weighed—a detail he wasn't sure it was wise to share.

"Congratulations!" Bernie said simply. "That's great."

Mrs. Pipkin stood smiling a moment longer, then suddenly seemed to remember they were all still standing in the entryway. "Well, come on in," she said, flipping her towel back over her shoulder. "We're almost ready to eat."

"The chicken smells good," Ben ventured as they followed her into the kitchen.

"You can tell your boss I didn't cheat on my diet," his mother informed Bernie proudly. "We're having barbecued chicken with the skin off, Slenderific baked beans, salad, and corn on the cob. How's that corn coming, honey?" she asked her husband.

Mr. Pipkin turned around at the sink, a half-shucked ear of corn in his hand, and Ben almost had a heart attack. His father was wearing a pink ruffled apron!

"Last one," he reported proudly, holding up the corn.

"Good. Honey, this is Benny's little—"

Ben squeezed his eyes shut, mortified.

"Uh, I mean Ben's friend, Bernie," Mrs. Pipkin corrected herself, to Ben's complete amazement.

Ben opened his eyes again. His dad was still wearing his mother's apron, but a guy couldn't have everything.

"Hello, Bernie," said Mr. Pipkin. "We've heard a lot about you."

"Same here," she returned. "Love your apron."

Ben froze. *He* knew Bernie was kidding. Would his dad?

"This isn't mine, it's my wife's," Mr. Pipkin explained earnestly. Then, miraculously, he caught the mischief in Bernie's eyes. "Oh, I get it. Maybe you'd like to wear it next."

Bernie giggled. "Maybe."

Mrs. Pipkin filled a pot with water for the corn. "I'm going to start this boiling now, which means we'll be eating in fifteen minutes. Ben, why don't you and Bernie go look at that new game your father's been working on?"

"Oh, you have to see this!" Ben exclaimed, towing Bernie into the den. Mr. Pipkin followed on their heels, eager to show off his latest. "My dad designs the best computer games."

"Ben told me about Tomb of Terror," Bernie informed Mr. Pipkin.

"He did, did he?" Mr. Pipkin laughed. "Did he tell you about Patch of Panic?"

"What?" she asked, puzzled.

"Yes, I did," Ben said, giving his dad a long-suffering look. "I told you I crashed all those hard drives at school. My dad had to write a patch program for me to give to everyone."

"Was that difficult?" Bernie asked Mr. Pipkin.

"Well, it took a while. But programming is really just simple steps. If you take enough in the right direction, eventually you cross the finish line."

He pulled out the chair in front of his computer and motioned for Bernie to sit down. She did, but her eyes stayed on him instead of the monitor.

"That's what I love about programming," she said. "It's all just logical, isn't it? One thing follows another, and if you don't end up where you want to be, you have no one to blame but yourself. Computers don't make accusations or treat anyone better than anyone else. Programming is like . . . the most fair thing in the world."

"Exactly!" exclaimed Mr. Pipkin.

Ben watched the smile that passed between them and finally let out his breath. They got each other. They really did.

Mr. Pipkin fired up his latest game, a futuristic simulation of a planetary space station. The colonists had to find water, plant crops, and ration food and medicine in order to survive until the transport ship came back. It sounded simple—until a player figured out that no matter how things were rationed, there weren't enough supplies to go around. That was when the real game began—the sneaking, the plotting, the coups. Interpersonal relations got

so ugly that it was almost a relief when the aster-
oids began crashing through the top of the biodome
and evil little space creatures started burrowing
up from beneath. And then there was the space
plague . . .

"This is amazing!" Bernie cried, impressed. "Look
at these graphics!"

"You've hardly seen anything yet," Ben said
proudly. "When the transport ship comes, they all
have to—"

"Dinner!" Mrs. Pipkin called.

"I'll show you the rest later," Ben promised.

In the dining room, dinner was already on the
table—a heaping platter of chicken surrounded
by bowls of baked beans, corn, and a fresh green
salad. Ben's mother had gone all out, and as he
took in the elaborate spread, Ben felt a rush of
pride.

"Everything looks great, Mom," he said, giving
her a grateful smile.

"Everything looks *terrific*," Bernie corrected. "Is
that the Slenderific barbecue sauce recipe?"

"Yes," said Mrs. Pipkin. "I hope it's good."

"It's really good," Bernie told her. "I have their
cookbook at home and I use it all the time. Their
recipes are so healthy."

"That's the main thing," Ben's mother said, pleased.
"Losing weight is nice, but being healthy . . . that's
what's important."

As they bent their heads for grace, Ben grinned at Bernie across the table. In fifteen minutes she'd not only charmed his mother and father, he was pretty sure she'd figured out where the trap door was to the space station's first subterranean level.

She truly was the perfect girl.

Eight

"Come on. It's just a little farther," Miguel urged, looking back over his shoulder.

Leah dragged her boots up the steep path behind him, her face pink with exertion. "I can't believe you wanted to go hiking today," she complained. "Don't you get enough of this stuff during the week?"

"I could never bring campers up here," he said. "Those kids complain about the trails around the lake, and the ground there is practically level compared to this."

"I noticed," Leah grumbled.

Miguel smiled. "Just a little farther," he promised again.

Minutes later they emerged from the woods onto a plateau higher than anything in front of them. The ridges of the Ozarks fell away into infinity, a sea of trees under a blue, blue sky.

"Oh, Miguel!" Leah gasped, running out to the edge of the bluff to get a better view. "It's beautiful!"

"I told you," he said proudly.

"But how did you know? I never even knew this place existed."

"My dad used to bring me, when I was younger." Miguel braced himself for the wrenching pain that typically accompanied any reference to his dead father, but for once it didn't come. The memory of those hikes was so precious that all he felt was a pang . . . and gratitude that they'd been able to take them. "He didn't bring Rosa, just me. It was our guy thing."

"I feel so honored," Leah teased. "Is there a secret handshake?"

"Very funny. Come on, there's a good place to sit over here."

He led her to a polished slab of rock near the edge of the bluff, swung his backpack off his shoulder, and motioned for her to sit beside him in the shade, where the rock wouldn't burn their bare legs. Opening his pack, he began taking out the picnic lunch he'd brought.

"You made us sandwiches?" Leah cried when she saw them. "All I brought was water."

"Good. Water's heavier," he said with a wink. He took out two individual bags of pretzels, two oranges, and a couple of marshmallow pies to add to their lunch. "Oops. These look kind of melted. Maybe chocolate wasn't such a good idea."

"Chocolate is *always* a good idea. I just wish you

had told me to bring something too. Now I feel guilty."

"Because I wanted to make you lunch?" Miguel shook his head. "Get over it."

"Well, I'll try," she said with a smile. "Especially if that ham has Dijon mustard on it."

"Would I give you any other kind?"

Miguel handed over the sandwich, pleased he had remembered about the mustard. After all, wasn't that what being in love meant? Knowing the details, caring about the small stuff? Anyone could instantly see that Leah was both intelligent and beautiful, but knowing what kind of mustard she liked . . . that type of thing took time.

She took a few contented bites, then sighed. "I can't believe we only have one more week together."

"I know."

The thought was there all the time, beneath everything they said and did. If he didn't bring it up as often as she did, that didn't mean it wasn't on his mind. It seemed summer had just started, and now it was nearly over.

"When are you and your mom leaving for California?" he asked. "Did she decide yet?"

Leah's sigh was bigger this time. She put down her half-eaten sandwich. "Monday. Not tomorrow," she added hurriedly, as if he hadn't already known that. "A week from tomorrow."

"Why so early?" he asked, trying not to whine. "I thought Stanford didn't start until mid-September."

"But CU starts in two weeks, and Mom has a full schedule of classes to teach. If we're going to drive all the way across country, get me unpacked, and get her on a plane back here in time, we have to leave on Monday."

"How many miles is it?" Miguel argued. "If you two trade off driving and sleeping, you'd never even have to stop. You could probably make it in three days."

"That's just not going to happen. My mom's turning it into this whole big thing—planning out a route on the map, picking a town to stay in each night. There are all these little places she's always been dying to see, and apparently this is her big chance. If things were different, a trip like that might be fun, but . . ." Her hazel eyes locked on his and he saw tears sparkling in her lashes. "I really wish I could just fly out myself the day I have to be there."

"But then you wouldn't have your car," he said, beginning to realize how hopeless it was.

"Or half my clothes, or the rest of my stuff for school."

He nodded and finished his sandwich without another word. Leah opened a bag of pretzels and began nibbling at those.

"I guess it's not *terrible* timing," he said at last. "I

mean, you'll be leaving town the same day everyone else goes back to CCHS."

"And what will you be doing? You'll still have a whole week off before you start at CU."

"I'll put in as many hours at the hospital as they'll let me. And then I'll work on the house. Stripping the kitchen cabinets is my next big project."

"Sounds fun." Her tone said the exact opposite.

"Yeah." For once, even he couldn't get that excited about the house. He peeled an orange while she stared into space, no longer seeing the view.

"I hate that we're splitting up!" she exclaimed, and the tears finally spilled over.

"What?" He dropped the orange abruptly. "We're *not* splitting up. Don't say that!"

"You know that's what's going to happen," she insisted, turning her tear-streaked face his way. "We'll make a bunch of promises, but it'll be too hard to keep them. Long-distance relationships never work."

"That's not true." No matter how upsetting, Miguel wasn't about to accept a temporary separation as the end of their relationship. "You just have to have a little faith," he said, putting his arms around her and pulling her close.

"In what?"

"In yourself!"

He still remembered too well how he had

proposed to her in January. In a rush of insecurity, he had convinced himself that if he let her out of his sight, things would be over between them. But he'd been wrong then . . . and they were even stronger now.

"It's not a question of faith in myself. Or even faith in you."

"No?" He squeezed her tightly, trying to force his confidence into her. "Then have some faith in us."

"Hey! What are you doing here?" Melanie called to Peter.

Putting down one foot, she stopped her bike outside the activities center at Clearwater Crossing Park. The sun was beating on the roof, but a tree near the doorway cast needed shade over the concrete stoop Peter had just walked out onto.

"I could ask you the same thing," he said, pushing his blond bangs out of his eyes. His chin was dripping sweat, and his T-shirt clung to his chest. "Why aren't you home in that nice big pool of yours?"

"I'm on my way," she admitted. Swinging her leg off the back of the bike, she laid the ten-speed down in the grass and joined Peter in the shade. "I thought it was a good day to get some exercise, but I didn't know it would be such a scorcher."

"You want exercise?" Peter offered, smiling. "You came to the right place!"

Turning around in the doorway, he walked back

into the activities center, where Melanie now saw individual-sized gymnastics mats spread out over the otherwise empty floor. The center's folding tables and chairs were stacked against the dais at the far end of the room, out of the way.

"Did you get all these mats out?" she asked. "What for?"

"I'm just wiping them down with disinfectant, making sure they're ready for when the Junior Explorers start coming back here on Saturdays. I'm planning gymnastics for our first weekend."

"Camp isn't even over yet and you're already worried about fall?"

"I kind of am," he admitted. "I'm not going to have Chris to help me this year, and with Jason moving in I'll probably be a lot busier at home. Not to mention school . . . Do you think senior year is a lot harder?"

"I doubt it. I know some complete idiots who graduated last year."

Peter laughed. "I hope you're right. I would hate it if I had to cut back on Junior Explorers." He had originally started the group with a partner, Chris Hobart, but Chris was about to be a senior in college and needed to move on.

"Why should you cut back when you have all of us to help you? Chris is out, but there's still Eight Prime." Melanie hesitated a moment, considering Leah and Miguel's situations. "Or six of us, anyway."

He nodded uncertainly. "It's just that it's a new year. And everyone's going to be busy with new things. . . ."

Melanie could tell he was genuinely worried, and not about himself. Peter was always thinking of other people first—then doing something to help them. Once again Melanie found herself struck with admiration for the quiet guy who gave so much to so many.

"We'll figure it out, Peter. I swear," she promised. "I'll be down here every Saturday myself, if you need me."

"Yeah?" he asked hopefully.

"Sure," she said with a mischievous smile. "After all, we juniors have practically nothing to do."

"I didn't say that!" he protested, laughing as she gave him a mock-offended push across the floor.

"So what's the story with these mats?" she asked. "Is there something I can help you do right now?"

"You can help me fold them up and stack them in the closet," he said eagerly. "They must be dry by now."

"Unless they're sweating too," she joked, pulling the front of her shirt away from her sticky body. "Hey, after this, why don't you come over and swim with me? Call Jenna, if you want."

"Don't tempt me," Peter said with a groan. He stooped to fold the nearest mat, flipping its rectangular sections into a neat stack. "I promised David I'd cut the grass. He was going to do it, but he and Caitlin . . ." Peter shrugged, an envious smile on his face. "It's the last weekend before the wedding, you know. I'd have better things to do too."

They stacked mats for a while in silence. Melanie folded and dragged them to the cupboard while Peter piled them inside. The mats were heavy and the strong-smelling disinfectant got up her nose as she pulled them through the warm, heavy air inside the activities center. Even so, her job was easy compared to Peter's. She watched as he heaved mat after mat up onto the growing stack, never uttering a word of complaint.

Where does he get the energy? She knew he would have already been to church that Sunday morning. Presumably he'd come straight from there to clean mats for the Junior Explorers, and in a few more minutes he'd be running home to cut grass in the blazing heat, just to give David more time with his fiancée. *The most amazing part is, he never seems to resent any of it. It's like the more he does, the stronger he gets.*

Melanie wondered if that were possible. Was there really some larger source of strength a person could tap into?

"You know what?" she blurted out as Peter lifted the last mat above his head. "I *will* go to that Bible class with you this fall. If you still want to, I mean."

He tossed the mat into position and turned around with a huge smile on his face. "Fantastic!" he said happily. "You're going to love Mrs. Fuerte."

You're the one I love, she thought, but she could never risk saying that. She'd been drawn to Peter right from the start, and for a while even she had confused it with something physical. Now she finally understood the true nature of the bond. She admired Peter as a person; she valued him as a friend; she respected him more than she'd have guessed possible. . . .

She loved him like the brother she'd never had.

"I'll put our names on the list this week," he said. "Will Jesse want to come too?"

Melanie shook her head. "Nah. But give him a couple weeks of missing me on that night, and who knows? Anything is possible."

Peter chuckled, the warmth of his laughter infectious. "That's what I keep telling you."

"Family meeting!" Mr. Brewster called from the bottom of the stairs.

Now what? thought Nicole, rolling over on her bed. They had barely arrived home from church and a long, boring brunch. All she wanted was to be left alone.

"Coming!" Heather called back from her bedroom. Two seconds later she was in Nicole's doorway.

"You're still wearing your church dress? You're going to get it wrinkled, lying around like that."

"Sue me," said Nicole, not moving.

Heather made a face. "I would if you had any money. Are you coming downstairs, or what?"

"Do I have a choice?" Nicole asked with a sigh.

She heaved herself reluctantly off the bed, wondering why she couldn't have just one single day to herself. One day in the week when she didn't have to go to school, or do volunteer work, or chores, or speak to people she didn't want to . . .

Even God said we were supposed to have a day off. Of course, then he went and filled up half of it for us, she thought, shuffling sullenly down the stairs. *It's not fair.*

In the living room, her parents had already hogged the armchairs; Nicole had to sit next to Heather on the sofa. She slumped across the cushions and yawned without covering her mouth, hoping her father would take the hint.

I don't know why Dad needs us all down here anyway, she thought, picking at a thread in the upholstery. *I haven't done anything wrong . . . and even Heather's been less obnoxious than usual. Besides, he didn't seem mad at brunch.*

On the contrary, he and Mrs. Brewster had been so gooey sweet to each other throughout the entire meal that Nicole had barely been able to eat.

"I have an important announcement to make," her father said proudly. "It's about the baby."

Heather scooted out to the edge of her seat. Even Nicole raised her head a bit.

"You know we wanted to be surprised as to whether it was a boy or a girl . . ." he continued.

Nicole's eyes darted questioningly to her mother. Mrs. Brewster already knew the baby was a boy, and so did Nicole. Her mother gave her a warning look. *Act surprised*, it said.

" . . . but it's a boy!" he said joyfully. "We wanted you girls to be the first to know."

I was, Nicole thought ironically, forgetting her fatigue enough to sit up.

"A boy! Oh, a brother!" Heather squealed delightedly. "It's a good thing we found out now, because almost all the names I've picked are for girls!"

"Your father has that covered," said Mrs. Brewster.

"Yep," he confirmed, grinning. "We're naming him Nicolas Heath Brewster, after you two girls."

"What?" A boy named for his sisters? Nicole had never heard of such a thing. "Dad, that's just not right! If he's going to be named for any of us, he ought to be named for you. Tell him, Mom."

But her father shook his head, his gray eyes gleeful behind his glasses. "The world will get by without one more Jimmy."

"Naming the baby for you girls was all your father's idea," Mrs. Brewster explained. "You ought to be honored."

Nicole was *too* honored, that was the problem. Tears welled up at the mere idea. That her father would name his only son after *her* . . .

Well, all right. Heather too. But my name's first.

"You should put Heath first," Nicole heard herself blurting out. "It's a cool name and not as common as Nick."

"Do you think so?" her mother asked. "Heath Nicolas. Nicolas Heath. I don't know. What do you think, Jimmy?"

"I like it!" Heather put in quickly.

"Sorry, squirt," said her father. "Those names are staying in the order they came in. No sane man messes with perfection."

"Perfection?" Nicole echoed weakly.

"That's right," he said, smiling at her and Heather. "We did pretty good with those names last time. And besides, it's like a circle. If I end up loving this baby just half as much as I love each of you, I'll love you all the same."

"Daddy!" Heather flung herself off the sofa and into his arms.

"I think there's something wrong with your math, Dad," Nicole objected weakly. She couldn't quite figure it out, though, and a second later she decided she didn't want to. She got up to hug her father too, tears finally spilling over at the enormity of having a new life named for her. "But I have to admit, it *sounds* pretty good."

"We're going to have the best time with this baby!" Heather exclaimed, clapping her hands with excitement. "Baby Heath!"

"Baby Nick!" Nicole corrected immediately.

"Baby Nicolas," their parents said in unison.

Everyone laughed, happy with the plan, and in the confusion that followed, Nicole found herself staring impatiently at her mother's belly.

October 31 just seemed like too long to wait for the little guy.

Nine

"It feels weird knowing this is the last week of camp," Jenna told Leah during crafts Monday morning. "It's even more weird with Jesse and Nicole already gone."

"Nicole has cheerleading practice all week," Belinda reported, pleased to have some inside information.

"That's right," Jenna confirmed. "And Jesse has football."

"Just wait until tomorrow, when Miguel goes to the hospital," said Leah. "Then things are really going to seem dead around here."

"Yeah."

Jenna watched the little girls busily making sun catchers in the cabin, coloring clear plastic ovals with markers. With Miguel out the next day, Jenna would have to take a group instead of teaching crafts, which had been her job through most of the summer. Considering that the last week of camp was a short one—ending on Thursday to give everyone an extra day off before school started—and that

Peter had a lot of special activities planned, there was a good chance Jenna wouldn't be teaching crafts again.

"I'll miss being Art Director," she sighed.

"There's always next summer." Leah sounded a bit envious.

"That's true," said Jenna, brightening. "And I can't wait for the wedding this weekend! You and Miguel are still coming, right?"

"We wouldn't miss it! Everyone's excited about hearing your new band."

Jenna was excited about that too. And then, only two days later, she'd be starting senior year. It almost didn't seem possible, the way summer had just blurred by. . . .

"Hey!" Leah shouted abruptly. "No coloring mustaches on each other!"

"What?" Jenna gasped, jolted out of her daydream. "You guys! Those are permanent markers!"

"Permanent?" Little Lisa Atwater looked horrified, and with good reason. The curly black mustachio on her upper lip clashed badly with her blond hair.

"Go wash your faces. Go!" Jenna cried, hustling everyone out of the cabin and pointing them toward the hose at the center of camp. "We need soap," she called back to Leah. "And paper towels!"

"On it," said Leah, emerging with a gooey bottle of dish soap left from the kids' camping trip and a crusty scrubber sponge. "This ought to take care of it."

"Are you kidding me?"

"It's all we've got." Leah glanced at the sponge, then laughed. "We'll tell them to pretend this is a fancy health spa and they're all going to have the deluxe exfoliating facial."

"I suppose if we don't rub very hard . . ."

"Or we can send them home the way they are and let their parents deal with them."

"Bring the sponge," Jenna decided quickly, imagining their parents' expressions. "What have we got to lose?"

"These running drills are killing me," Gary Baldwin complained, hugging his ribs tight and bending forward across his arms. "Do you think Coach could have found a *hotter* day to do this?"

Jesse smiled, resigned to the heat he had hated so intensely the summer before. He was dripping with sweat—the entire football team was—but he wasn't out of breath. "What's killing you is the fact that you sat on your butt all summer eating bonbons."

"Very funny," Gary grunted. "Just because I'm not running around with my shirt off, like Mr. Physique."

"You would if you could," said Jesse, flexing his six-pack abs. "Eat your heart out, Baldwin."

A whistle sliced through the humidity on the CCHS football field, signaling the end of the drill.

Players started trotting back to line up for the next one.

"I can't do it," Gary said, still panting. "I mean, who really needs to be a starter anyway? I'd rather come in after the other team is tired from beating the crap out of you guys."

At the far end of the field, Coach Davis opened a big mesh bag and began tossing out footballs.

"Finally!" Jesse exclaimed, unable to hide his excitement. "He's breaking out the balls. Let's go!"

Jesse sprinted down the field without waiting for Gary to follow. His feet raced over the grass, heels flying up behind him. He was in shape, he was in love, and football was about to start.

What more could a guy want? he thought, stretching out his hands for a ball.

The coach lobbed him an easy pass. Jesse tucked it under one arm as he blasted past the other players, looping around them at top speed. Even when he finally stopped, he wasn't out of breath.

"Been eating your Wheaties, Jones?" the coach asked dryly.

"Something like that," Jesse said, grinning. No matter how unimpressed Coach acted, Jesse knew he was taking notes.

"All right. Let's get out there and toss the ball around," Coach Davis directed, clapping his hands. "Loosen up those arms for some passing drills."

Jesse paired off with the nearest person, a junior who was making his debut on varsity. From earlier introductions, Jesse remembered the guy's name was Drew. Judging by his build, he played defense.

"Where did the cheerleaders go?" Drew wondered aloud as he and Jesse lobbed short passes to each other.

"Don't know," Jesse grunted, concentrating on his spiral. The girls had been on the field when the team had first shown up, but Sandra had moved them, first to the sidelines and then out of the area altogether. If Melanie had stayed on the squad, Jesse might have been more interested in their whereabouts, but he could see Nicole anytime.

The ball went back and forth.

"It's no fun playing without an audience," Drew complained.

"Better not let Coach hear you say that."

Drew glanced wistfully into the stands. A few girlfriends and wannabe girlfriends were scattered throughout the bleachers, but practices would draw much larger crowds once school started again. And then there were the games . . .

Jesse imagined running onto the field for the first game of the season, greeted by a thousand screaming fans. Small-town Clearwater Crossing took its high school football seriously—and so did he.

Drew caught the ball and held it. "Here come

some likely-looking ladies," he said, his eyes fixed on a point over Jesse's shoulder.

Jesse turned around and almost died of embarrassment. Brittany and one of her teenybopper friends were walking down the sideline, practically on the field.

"Go, Jesse!" she yelled when she saw him looking, waving her hands overhead as if they held pompoms. Both girls were wearing tight camisoles over nearly flat chests, their skinny legs made even longer by platform sandals.

"I think someone has a crush on you," Drew said, his voice slick with insinuation.

"Give me a break. She's in eighth grade," said Jesse, pained.

Drew shrugged. "I'd do her."

Jesse charged so quickly that Drew hit the grass on his back before he could have guessed what was coming. Jesse knelt on the other boy's chest, one hand tightening around Drew's throat, the other cocked back in a fist just inches from his face.

"That's my *sister*, you pervert," he spat, so angry that little black spots floated through his vision.

Drew's hands came to his face, palms up in a gesture of peace. "All right. Who knew? How about getting off me now?"

Jesse hesitated, then backed slowly off his adversary. He still felt like pounding the guy to a pulp, but if he did, Coach Davis would bench him for sure.

"You'd better watch what you say about people's sisters," he warned, still glaring.

"Yeah. Whatever." Drew picked up the ball. "They're all *somebody's* sister," he muttered as he walked off.

For a moment, Jesse considered tackling him again. Drew wasn't expecting a hit, and he was soft on top of that. He'd be facedown eating grass before he suspected a thing.

"Jesse!" Brittany called again, her voice embarrassingly high. "Jesse, over here!"

Jesse abandoned his murderous thoughts against Drew and wheeled to face his sister.

"Good tackle!" she said, clapping. She obviously had no idea that his altercation with Drew hadn't been part of the drill.

"What do you want?" he demanded angrily. "You're not even supposed to be here."

Brittany's face fell. She glanced nervously at her friend, clearly embarrassed by his reaction.

"I wanted to introduce you to Bethany," she said, a pleading tone in her voice. "We met at the mall. She goes to Samuel Clemens."

"Wow," he said sarcastically. "Thank God you interrupted me at practice for that."

Bethany stared down at her pink-painted toenails, making him feel like a jerk.

"Look, I'm sorry. Great to meet you, Bethany. Okay? But I'm kind of busy here." He gestured behind him to the rest of the team, many of whom were now openly watching the girls. "You guys aren't helping me out with Coach."

"I only wanted you to see that I *do* have a friend at Samuel Clemens now," Brittany said quickly. "So if you could just tell Mom . . ."

"This again?" he said impatiently. "Look, Brittany, get out of here. I mean it. I don't want you on the field."

Coach Davis blew his whistle to end the drill.

"I guess I can be on the field if I want to," Brittany retorted.

"Go home. I'm not kidding."

She started to put her hands on her hips, then abruptly reconsidered. "Will you talk to Mom?"

"Only if you leave right now."

Walking back to the huddle, though, Jesse wasn't so sure he'd keep that promise. How could Brittany be so stupid as to show up on a football field, dressed like that, and expect guys not to notice? Granted, she was young—but did she have to be clueless, too?

She's not clueless, she's just that innocent, he realized. *She has no idea what pigs guys can be.*

Part of him wondered how she was ever going to learn. The rest of him didn't want her to have to.

Maybe Elsa has a point. Maybe Brittany should stay in Catholic school.

*   *   *

118

Smith sucked air through her coffee-stained teeth, a sound that stretched Melanie's nerves to the breaking point.

"What now?" she cried, stomping on the brake. The student car came to an abrupt halt in the middle of the otherwise empty parking lot. "What did I do wrong now?"

"You're too close to the left side of the space," Smith said. "You're at least four inches off center."

"Four inches?" Melanie repeated disbelievingly. She'd been practicing parking between the angled white lines of a typical parking lot for at least half an hour. Even in the spaces marked for compact cars, she was stopping well between the lines every time. "Are you sure? Maybe you'd like to get out and measure," she invited sarcastically.

Smith's grizzled head whipped around. Her gray eyes narrowed dangerously. "Maybe *you'd* like to get out and measure. Go ahead."

Melanie's heart leapt up and lodged somewhere near her windpipe. She could feel it beating in her throat. "That's okay. I—"

"I insist. Get out and check."

Her sweaty hand slipped on the door handle as Melanie exited the car and stepped onto the steaming pavement. It was past five o'clock that Tuesday, but the sun was still blazing overhead and the black-top stank of melting tar. She walked nervously to the front of the car, then stood staring back at it, trying to judge how well it was centered in the space.

That's right in the middle! she thought, frustrated. *Or maybe just barely to the left. Barely. A couple, three . . . four inches.*

Great.

Smith was right. Wouldn't she just love that?

The woman had it in for her. All lesson long the driving instructor had either criticized or made fun of every single thing Melanie had done. The idea of encouragement was obviously completely foreign to her. And now—the one time Melanie had dared to take her on—Smith turned out to be right.

This is bad, she thought, walking back to the car. *I'm never going to get my license.*

"Well? What did you see?" Smith demanded as Melanie slid behind the wheel.

"It's a little to the left," Melanie admitted, not looking at her teacher. Smith was slightly less scary when kept to peripheral vision.

"Yeah. About four inches to the left," Smith gloated. "You have to listen, Miss Andrews. Why do you think your father hired me?"

I must have done something very, very bad that I'm completely unaware of, Melanie answered silently.

"Because I know driving!" Smith declared. "I can drive anything, anytime. And let me tell you something: All those years of giving driving tests to morons made me realize what a truly rare skill that is."

"Oh," Melanie whispered, pulling the car out of the space and driving around in a loop to try again.

"When you're driving, you can't be too precise," Smith continued, warming to her lecture. "You need to know exactly where every part of your car is at all times—unless you want to hit something, of course."

"Uh-huh." Melanie was barely listening as she lined up on a new space.

"Maybe you think I'm being too particular . . . and with this rusted-out piece of junk, maybe I am. But get behind the wheel in that Hummer of yours and everything's gonna change. Four inches in that beast is going to be the difference between being between the lines and being in the next space."

Melanie held her breath and parked, wondering why Smith felt the need to mention the Hummer every two minutes.

So I'm going to be driving a Hummer. We both know I'll be driving a Hummer. But I won't be driving a Hummer with her.

The plan was for Melanie to take her driving test in the practice car, and after that it was *adios*, Smith.

Why can't she just concentrate on what we're actually doing?

"That's better," Smith said grudgingly, peering out the car window. "You're probably only two inches off this time. Try again."

Melanie pulled wordlessly out of the space, trying again. And again. And again. As far as she could tell, she was parking perfectly, but Smith was down to worrying about millimeters now.

"It's a shame we aren't practicing with the Hummer," she said. "Then you'd see what I'm talking about. That car could crush this one like an empty can."

If this car's such junk, why are we driving it? Melanie wondered irritably, but she didn't dare sass Smith again.

"I'm sure my dad will bring me out here and let me practice parking the Hummer with him," she said instead.

"Yes, well . . . that will have to do." Smith checked her watch. "We have eleven minutes left. I suppose we can't put off parallel parking any longer. We'll start over there."

She pointed to the far side of the parking lot, where a long concrete curb separated the edge of the pavement from the adjacent landscaping. Spaces were marked at an angle to the curb, but the entire stretch of them was empty.

"Parallel parking. That's what separates the men from the boys," Smith announced as Melanie rolled tentatively toward the curb. "You wouldn't believe how many drivers I flunked over parallel parking!"

I'll bet I would. Melanie's hands were starting to sweat again.

"Of course, this is all going to be wasted effort

once you start driving the Hummer. You probably won't even be able to *see* the curb from where you sit in that thing."

"Why do you keep bringing up the Hummer?" Melanie blurted out in frustration. "Why can't we just drive *this* car?"

Smith drew back in her seat, offended. "I *don't* keep bringing it up," she said icily. "I'm simply making a point—a *driving* point. That's what your father pays me for."

"Oh."

"If you don't think my instruction is relevant, perhaps you'd like to find another teacher." Smith's gray eyebrows had risen almost into her hair.

"No, that's okay," Melanie mumbled quickly. If she fired Smith, her father would never hire her another driving teacher—and then she'd definitely never get her license.

Not that it's looking too likely anyway. At this rate, I'll have an untouched Hummer sitting in the driveway until I'm twenty.

"That's *okay?*" Smith repeated, her voice dripping acid.

"I mean, I'm sorry," said Melanie, practically in tears. "I just don't want to think about the Hummer yet, when I don't even have my license. I need to concentrate on one thing at a time."

Smith's mouth twisted into an evil smile. "You

need to concentrate, all right. You got that part straight."

Melanie blinked hard as she braked near the curb, trying to keep from crying.

I'll be the last person left in Missouri who's not allowed to drive!

Ten

"I have to go," said Courtney, glancing at her watch. "I promised my mom I'd be home by four-thirty."

"But I just got here!" Nicole protested. "We've only been to one store!"

She had practically killed herself rushing from cheerleading practice to the back-to-school sales at the mall, and now Courtney was already leaving? Why had she bothered?

Courtney shrugged. "Sorry. But after I talked to you this morning, my mom told me we're supposed to go to some sort of barbecue at the new neighbors' house. I can't miss it—that would be rude."

Nicole had a feeling that what Courtney thought would be rude was missing a chance to socialize with the mysteriously dark and handsome teenage boy she'd been spying on from her second-story window, but Court didn't give her a chance to argue.

"Anyway, Gail can stay and shop with you, right, Gail?" Courtney asked, turning to Nicole's cousin.

"Then you can drive her home, Nicole, and save me a trip to Mapleton."

"But—but—" Nicole sputtered, too outraged to come up with a good excuse.

Given the nasty way Gail had been treating her since they'd started speaking again, the last thing Nicole wanted was to spend time alone with her cousin. Not only that, but she couldn't help suspecting Courtney had manipulated the whole situation just to avoid making the forty-five minute round-trip to Gail's house.

"That's right, cuz. I'm all yours." Gail threw an arm across Nicole's shoulders and leaned on her with an uncomfortable amount of weight.

Oh boy, Nicole thought sarcastically.

Courtney was already making her escape. "I'll see you guys later," she called, waving, from twenty feet away. "Don't do anything I wouldn't do!"

"She has no idea how likely that is," Nicole muttered with a sideways glance at Gail.

"Really, cuz. I'm hurt," Gail said, steering Nicole in a semicircle and dragging her off in the opposite direction. "You think I'm that much trouble?"

Nicole chewed her lip, then made a decision. There were a couple of things she'd been dying to tell Gail, and this was her big chance. "I don't think it, I know it," she said with conviction.

Gail's arm dropped off her shoulders. She faced Nicole in the crowded mall courtyard, a trace of ice in her blue eyes. "You're the one who got us fired from our jobs."

"*You* got fired. *I* quit." Nicole's voice was loud enough to turn heads, but she'd been stuffing her resentment down for so long that she barely even cared. Once she had felt guilty about the Wienerageous incident, but Gail's behavior since she'd reappeared had more than cured her of that. Without Courtney there as a buffer, Nicole was finally free to say what she liked.

"What does that prove?" Gail demanded. "Only that you're a bigger goody-goody than I'll ever be."

"Shut up! If you weren't stealing food, none of that would have happened. You could still be working at that greasy dive, kissing Mr. Roarke's butt. Or wait." Nicole pretended to think. "That's what got you in trouble last time."

Her cousin's eyes turned positively glacial. "At least men find me attractive. You couldn't even hold on to Noel for three months."

"Because I didn't want to! I broke up with Noel!"

"If you hadn't, I'd have taken him from you. It wouldn't even have been a challenge."

"Oh yeah?" Nicole was beside herself. "Apparently it *was* a challenge, because you did your best at Melanie's party and nothing happened, did it?"

"You don't know what happened."

"I don't *care* what happened!" Nicole practically screamed. "If you think Noel's so great, why don't you go call him? Do it right now. I'll give you his number!"

"Noel? Great?" Gail's lip curled with disdain. "I think he's the most shallow, boring, conceited guy I ever met. Loser with a capital L. He ought to come with a warning label to keep normal girls from wasting their time."

Nicole was stunned. But even though Gail was right, she couldn't let her get away with saying that. After all, Nicole had been the loser's girlfriend.

"What about that loser Neil that *you* were so in love with?" she flung back. "If I saw that guy in an alley, I'd run for the police. I'll bet they'd know him too."

"You're an idiot, Nicole. If you didn't judge every book by its cover, you might have noticed that Neil was smart, and fun, and he *loved* me. If you weren't so blinded by looks, you *might* have noticed that Noel is a subintelligent user who doesn't even like you very much!"

Nicole felt as if she'd just stepped off the edge of a cliff. How could Gail be so mean and so smart both in the same breath? And if she saw through Noel so easily, what must she see when she looked at Nicole?

Nicole swallowed hard, trying to find her voice. "Maybe you're right. A little. About Noel." She glanced behind her and noticed an empty bench a few feet away. Backing up, she sat down abruptly, her legs simply giving out.

"I'm right about Neil, too," Gail said, sitting beside her. Her eyes had thawed a bit, but her expression was still intense. "You ruined everything, Nicole."

"Me?" Nicole objected. "You said he'd had you long enough!"

"What am I supposed to say? That he was mad about me seeing Mr. Roarke? That after you got me fired, he decided he was too old for a girl whose parents could still ground her?"

Gail's voice had gone from angry to choky, and tears pooled in her eyes. "I *loved* him, Nicole. All the guys since then . . . Doug . . . all of them . . . were nothing but substitutes. I looked for guys who were even harder than Neil, just to freak my parents out worse, but none of them meant anything." Gail buried her face in her hands. "You should have just left me alone."

"I was trying to help you," said Nicole, starting to feel guilty again.

"But you can't!" her cousin told her, raising a tear-streaked face. "Don't you see? *Nobody* can help me. Sometimes . . ." Gail shook her head, her eyes fixed on some distant spot. "Sometimes I don't even want to be helped. It would be easier if this was all over."

Her cousin's words gave Nicole a sick feeling. "If what was all over?"

"This! All of it! Sometimes I wish I were dead."

Oh, my God, thought Nicole. *Is she serious? And what am I supposed to say?*

"I, uh . . . I know you loved Neil," she ventured at last, laying an uncertain hand on her cousin's back. "I mean, I know that *now*. But no guy's worth dying for. Right? And . . . well . . ." Inspiration struck. "He couldn't have been that great if he was dumb enough to leave you."

"He's *older* than I am, Nicole," sobbed Gail. "A lot older. It's not his fault."

"It's even *more* his fault, because he didn't have someone making his decisions for him, the way you did. If *his* parents—"

"No, stop. You just don't get it." Gail's eyes snapped back into focus and found Nicole's. "I'm not some lovesick teenager. This isn't all about Neil anymore. I'm just depressed, Nicole. I'm tired, and hopeless, and I just don't see the point. I haven't for a long time. Maybe if your life weren't so perfect, you'd know what I'm talking about."

"My life? Perfect?" squeaked Nicole. "If you knew anything about my life, you'd never be able to say that."

"And if you knew anything about mine, you'd know everything is relative." Gail's gaze flicked out over the mall again. She sounded totally defeated.

"But . . . I don't understand," said Nicole, beginning to feel a little desperate. "What's wrong with your life? Your parents love you and—"

"They don't even know me! Nobody does."

"I know you."

"No you don't." Gail's head dropped back into her fingers. "Sometimes I wish I could just kill myself."

Fear turned Nicole's heart to ice; she could barely catch her breath. "You have to tell someone, Gail. Really. You have to tell your parents."

"I'm not going to *do* it," Gail said irritably. "And I already made the mistake of telling my parents. They've been dragging me to shrinks and ministers ever since, like some sort of total head case. Why do you think they made me go to that stupid retreat where I met Courtney?"

"You said it was to get you away from Doug."

"I say a lot of things." Gail stood up abruptly, dashing the final tears from her eyes and squaring up her shoulders. "Listen, let's just forget it, okay? Life's too short for this crap."

"No! I don't want to forget it." The sight of Gail trying to deny so much pain brought Nicole to tears herself. In a rush, she remembered how tight the two of them had grown at Wienerageous, remembered how awful she'd felt when she'd believed her cousin would hate her for life. . . .

Leaping to her feet, Nicole threw her arms around Gail's neck. "You have to promise me you won't do anything to hurt yourself."

"Promise *you*?" Gail tried to wriggle free. "What for?"

"Because I love you!" cried Nicole, her arms tightening to a choke hold and her tears falling everywhere. "I didn't know how much before, but I really, really do."

"This is it," Peter said. "Are you ready?"

"Yes!" Jason answered, his blue eyes shining.

Peter had just parked in the Altmanns' driveway, having driven the two of them straight home from camp. David, stuck driving the Junior Explorers' bus to the park, wouldn't be home for another half hour, but Mr. Altmann's truck was parked in the open garage.

"Dad must have taken off early," said Peter. "I'll bet he wanted to be home when you got here."

Jason reached for the car door handle, then froze. Dirty sneakers tapped a rhythm on the dusty floor mat, the cadence becoming more agitated with every beat.

"What's the matter?" asked Peter.

"I'm scared," Jason admitted.

"Scared of what?"

"What if they don't like me?"

Peter burst out laughing. "Jason, they *already* like you. Mom and Dad did everything they could think of to get you moved in with us so fast. You're part of the family now."

"For real?" he asked nervously.

"Do brothers lie to brothers?" Peter's own excitement was almost unbearable. "Come on, let's go in.

Mom and Dad must have heard us pull up, and the suspense is probably killing them."

He and Jason climbed out of the car, swinging well-used backpacks over their shoulders. Peter was reaching for the front door when it suddenly flew open.

"You're here!" Mrs. Altmann cried, her husband beaming over her shoulder. "I'm so happy to see you, Jason. I thought camp would never be over today!"

She stepped forward to hug him, but Jason drew back quickly, and with an obvious effort, she restrained herself. The new social worker had warned them to go easy on the physical contact at first.

"It seemed long to me, too," said Peter.

Ever since they'd gotten the go-ahead the day before, all he'd been able to think about was this moment, when he'd finally bring Jason home. The adults had decided the transition would be less traumatic if Mrs. Brown said her good-byes in the morning and sent Jason to camp as usual, letting him come home with Peter in the afternoon. Jason had been sad earlier—Mrs. Brown had been good to him—but by lunchtime he'd been over it, itching to start his new life. Now that the moment had come, though, he stood rooted in the doorway, wide-eyed and tongue-tied.

"Mrs. Brown came by a while ago and dropped off your things, Jason," Mr. Altmann told him. "We've been arranging them in your new room. Want to see?"

Jason nodded.

"Come on, then," said Peter, breaking the human logjam in the entryway by pulling Jason down the hall. "Here's my bedroom," he said as they passed it, "and this very next door is yours!"

He pushed it open. Both boys walked in and stood there, transfixed.

"Jason!" Peter said at last. "You have a lot of stuff!"

Toys and sports equipment spilled out of boxes in every corner of the room, the open closet was stuffed with clothes, and several new pictures now hung on the walls. Knickknacks and a clock shaped like a baseball had been added to the desk, along with a photograph of a much younger Jason posing with a blond man and woman. The shelves were overrun with books, most of them in such pristine shape that they couldn't have been read, and on David's old bed the new blue comforter had been fluffed and smoothed to perfection, complete with matching pillow shams.

"Cool!" Jason said, falling backward onto the bed and rolling around as if his clothes weren't filthy.

Peter's parents appeared in the doorway. "Do you like it?" Mrs. Altmann asked anxiously.

"Yes!" Jason bolted up off the bed, passed them all

near the doorway, and ran a few feet down the hall. "And this is your room?" he asked Peter, hesitating by the open door.

Before Peter could answer, he darted in, then flew out again. "We're so close!" he crowed, running back into his own room and flinging himself, shoes and all, onto the new comforter.

Peter's mother cringed, but she didn't say anything.

"Yep, only a wall between us," Peter confirmed. "This used to be David's room, you know, but he moved his stuff out early so you could have it right away."

Peter and his mother had both insisted that Jason could sleep in Peter's room until after the wedding, but David had been equally determined to bunk out in the den. "Let Jason have his new room," he'd said. "We don't want to look like we aren't ready for him. Besides, the kid's had enough moves in his life."

"Where *is* David?" Jason asked, sitting up. "I thought he'd be here by now."

"He'll be here pretty soon." Mr. Altmann checked his watch. "Oops! If we're grilling burgers for dinner, I'd better get that charcoal started." He walked off down the hall in the direction of the back door.

"While he's doing that, let's get your camp stuff taken care of, Jason," Mrs. Altmann suggested.

"What do you mean?"

135

"Well, you have a wet bathing suit and towel, right? Where are they?"

"Oh." Jason got off the bed, opened his backpack, and dumped both wet, sandy articles onto the freshly vacuumed carpet. "There."

Peter choked back a chuckle.

"Um, good. I put a hamper right here in your closet." Mrs. Altmann picked up the nasty towel and dropped it quickly into the new wicker hamper. "Peter will show you how to rinse out your suit in the bathtub and hang it up to dry."

"Remember the bathroom we washed up in last time you were here?" Peter asked. "You and I will share that one now."

"Okay." Jason sat down where his towel had been only moments before and pulled off a shoe without untying its laces. "Look how much sand I got in here!" he bragged, pouring it out in a granular stream that mounded up on the carpet. "I'll bet there's twice as much in the other one!"

"Then let's take it off outside," Mrs. Altmann said quickly. "Whenever we have dirt in our shoes, we empty them in the yard."

Jason looked as if he thought she must be kidding.

Mrs. Altmann smiled. "I know you're used to doing things a certain way, Jason, and I don't expect you to learn all at once, but we Altmanns have our own system. Peter will show you where to empty your shoes, and then I want you boys to wash up for

136

dinner." She smiled again before she walked off down the hall. "It's good to have you home, Jason."

Jason's thrilled smile was even broader than hers as he brought his lips to Peter's ear. "*I'm* going to be an Altmann," he whispered. "And *she's* going to be my mother!"

Eleven

"Three cheers for Camp Clearwater!" Jenna rallied the campers from her place in front of the benches. "Hip, hip, hooray! Hip, hip, hooray! Hip, hip, hooray!"

Leah stood to the side, watching as the children cheered. Over at the flagpole, Peter had begun lowering the Camp Clearwater flag for the last time, signifying the end of summer camp.

How did it get to be Thursday so fast? Leah wondered miserably, her eyes slowly filling with tears. She had vowed to milk every minute of the last week, and now it was already gone. Her tears spilled over and ran down her cheeks, forcing her to wipe them with her hands.

She wasn't the only one crying, either. As the cheering came to an end, some of the kids started sniffling, and a few began sobbing openly with the realization that camp had just ended.

Ben jumped up on the end of a bench. "How about 'Row, Row, Row Your Boat'? In rounds!" he proposed, waving his hands above his head to catch the kids' attention. "You guys know how to do it now. Come on, and make me proud!"

To Leah's surprise, they launched right into it with him, singing their little hearts out. Ben's perseverance in the song department had finally paid off. The girls lifted sweet soprano voices, while the boys competed with each other to see who could sing the loudest. Some of the other counselors joined in, but Leah couldn't sing past the lump in her throat. She could hardly bear to think that camp was ending now, when they finally had things under such good control. . . .

"How are you holding up?" asked Miguel, appearing at her side. "You look kind of funny."

"I *feel* kind of funny," she choked out. "This is so sad."

Miguel shrugged. "I know. But it had to end sometime, right? Everything does."

He meant well, but he definitely wasn't helping. Two more tears ran down Leah's cheeks.

"It's not like anyone's dying," he insisted, putting a hand on her shoulder and leaning in close. "Besides, Jenna's passing out the ice cream now."

"She is?"

The counselors had all pitched in to treat the kids to ice cream bars as a going-away present. Even Jesse and Nicole had contributed, despite the fact that they couldn't be there. As Jenna lifted the lid on the cooler, fog from the dry ice rose up and flowed over its edge, causing a wave of excitement among the kids.

"Okay," she called out. "Everyone can come up for ice cream, one group at a time. . . ." She was almost buried under the stampede that followed as forty pushing, shoving kids charged her at once.

Leah chuckled in spite of her sadness. Maybe Eight Prime didn't have camp down quite so perfectly after all.

"That's the spirit," Miguel encouraged her, giving her shoulder a squeeze.

The two of them waded into the fray to rescue Jenna, while Peter and Melanie folded the flag and Ben jumped from bench to bench, futilely trying to distract the kids with another song. At last all the campers had ice cream. The noise and shouting gave way to an almost eerie quiet as the wrappers were stripped and the licking began.

"Too bad we couldn't have afforded ice cream every day," Peter joked as he and Melanie rejoined the group with the folded flag.

Melanie giggled. "We could have made it its own activity. I'll bet some of these kids could eat ice cream for at least two hours."

Jenna passed the last few ice cream bars around to the counselors. Peter asked her to save one for David, who had gone to air out the bus for the long, hot drive home.

The end of camp is no big deal for David, Leah

thought, licking melted ice cream off her fingers. *He's probably glad, in fact, with the wedding coming this weekend. . . .*

Her stomach twisted with unhappiness, refusing to be comforted by food. She went and found a trash bag, dropped in her half-eaten bar, and began picking up the sticky wrappers the kids had scattered everywhere. Soon sticks started hitting the ground as well, in spite of Jenna's repeated requests to put them in the trash can. The kids were wired now, bundles of frenzied energy playing tag around the benches and saying happy good-byes to their friends.

"Let's start heading for the bus!" Peter yelled, and his words were greeted by cheers. The kids grabbed their backpacks and began running for the trail so quickly that Jenna, Melanie, Ben, and Miguel were forced to sprint along with them in an attempt to keep some order. Leah was left behind with her garbage bag, in no mood to run anyway.

"Don't worry about the trash, Leah," Peter told her, hurrying past with Jason glued to his side. "I'll get out here in the next couple of days to make sure the place is clean and the cabin is boarded up for the year."

She nodded mutely, not trusting her voice, as Peter walked away. Her right hand clenched down on a bundle of gooey ice cream sticks and wrappers until her fingers hurt. At last she stuffed the mess into her trash bag, tied off its top, and went to retrieve her backpack. She was the last one left in the clearing, but she took her time anyway, rinsing her hands at the hose, and when she finally reached the trailhead, she turned to look behind her.

The flagpole stood lonely and bare beside benches that wouldn't see action for months. The big central oak seemed to brood. The lake and wooden dock looked as inviting as ever, though, and the sun still shone overhead, glinting off every tiny ripple. Only the calendar said summer was over. Aside from some arbitrary date, nothing had really changed. There didn't seem to be any good reason that everything had to end. Leah shifted her gaze from the lake to the cabin, where she'd spent so many happy hours doing crafts, making lemonade, helping her girls change for swimming. . . .

A surge of fresh tears blurred the pine green cabin into the woods behind it. She would never do any of those things again. And it wasn't just camp she'd be missing either. It was her hometown, and her family, and her friends. . . .

Leah turned abruptly, the trail swimming beneath her feet.

How can I ever leave all this behind?

"Well, at least you made it through the obstacle course without killing anyone," Smith said begrudgingly as Melanie pulled into the Andrewses' driveway after Thursday's lesson. "Assuming you don't count traffic cones."

"I don't."

Melanie was exhausted. The last day of camp had been draining enough without ending it with a dose of Smith. For the past hour the self-professed driving genius had had Melanie weaving the training car between orange cones like some sort of wheeled slalom skier, completely refusing to explain what pertinence the drill had to anything in the real world. They had done it at higher and higher speeds, streaking across the empty parking lot with the back end almost fishtailing, until Melanie could make the pass like an action hero.

The student car rolled to a stop beside the Hummer. Melanie put on the parking brake and started to get out.

"Doesn't it just kill you to see that beauty sitting there day after day when you're not allowed to drive it?" Smith asked.

"Yes." *Thanks for reminding me*, Melanie thought sullenly.

"Let's take it for a spin."

"Excuse me?"

"Drive it around town. Don't you want to?"

"I'm not *allowed* to," Melanie reminded her. "My father would kill me."

A brief peek into the open garage revealed that

he hadn't come home from work yet, but still . . . no way was she taking that chance. What if something went wrong?

"Sure. But he can't have anything against *me* driving it." Smith's voice was oily in its unaccustomed smoothness. Her lips stretched into a rusty smile. "I mean, after all, he hired me to teach you to drive, and there are probably a lot of tips I could give you if I got behind the wheel."

To Melanie's surprise, she was tempted. Her father kept promising to take her out in the Hummer, but as busy as he'd been lately, they'd only gone one time. She was undeniably eager to ride in her new car again—even if that meant putting Smith behind the wheel.

"Except that our hour is over," she said cautiously.

"Yeah, well . . . We won't be gone that long." Smith stretched her smile till it creaked. "Have you got a set of keys?"

The next thing Melanie knew, they were climbing into the Hummer. "I don't know if we should be doing this," she said anxiously. "I hope my dad doesn't get mad."

"No reason why he should," Smith said confidently. "This is good experience for you, and I'm not even charging him."

She turned the key in the ignition, a glint coming into her eyes at the powerful roar of the engine. She revved the motor a few times, increasing Melanie's nervousness, then backed the Hummer onto the Andrewses' private road.

She's not going to hit anything, Melanie reassured herself over and over, her hands twisting in her lap as Smith made speedy S-curves down the empty pavement. *She thinks she's such a great driver, she'd die if she hit anything.*

"Sweet," Smith breathed. "This baby really handles!"

Melanie tried to smile as if her heart weren't in her throat. Smith pulled onto the public road, one hand on the wheel, the other exploring every button on the instrument panel.

"You've got your headlights here, and your brights," she said, demonstrating for Melanie's benefit. "This here's your wipers, and your horn." She honked the horn once, then again, seemingly just for the heck of it. Melanie didn't remind her that they'd been over all those things in the driveway.

"Acceleration is good. Brakes . . . good," Smith announced, stomping on them at the intersection. "Listen to that engine purr!"

Melanie nodded weakly, but after a few more blocks rolled by, she'd forgotten her reservations. Smith had not only reverted to driving normally, she was in a far better mood than Melanie had ever seen or imagined.

"Let's just cruise by the park," she said, steering in that direction without waiting for a reply. "You've got to love the way this thing rides. I feel like I'm ten feet tall!"

"I know what you mean," said Melanie, looking out her window at the pavement streaking by beneath them.

"Sweet," Smith said again. "Listen, when you take the driving test, be sure to use your turn signal before you pull out of the examination station onto the street. I can't tell you how many people I've dinged for that. They think the test hasn't started yet, but don't make the same mistake. It starts the second the examiner walks out to the car."

"I—I'll remember that," Melanie said, surprised by the unexpected gift. Not that she expected it to help. Smith had told her during every lesson what a hopeless driver she was. If she ever managed to pass the test—some far-distant day down the road—it would be by the skin of her teeth.

"Yeah, do. And the speed limit right there is thirty-five. Everyone screws that up because they're so nervous they don't see the sign. Don't lose points on that type of trivia."

"Okay." In her mind, Melanie was already composing a chant: *turn signal, go thirty-five, turn signal, go thirty-five*. She repeated it over and over, determined to remember the only two clues Smith had ever given her.

"The other big weeder is parallel parking, but I'm pretty sure you've got that down."

Even Melanie was pretty sure of that. They'd done it at least three hundred times, and on both the left and right sides of the car, in case Melanie ever had to park on a one-way street.

"The main things are to watch your speed, signal every turn, stop completely, and for God's sake, stay in your own lane."

Melanie could fishtail through traffic cones. None of the things Smith was telling her now sounded very challenging.

"Look at this CD changer!" Smith said, poking at the buttons. "How many CDs can you put in here?"

"I don't know. I haven't used it yet."

"Well, what does the owner's manual say?"

"I don't know."

"You haven't read it?"

"I started to, but it's kind of long and . . . boring."

Smith shook her head, but, amazingly, didn't lecture. "Oh yeah!" she added instead. "When you pull back into the station after the test, set the parking brake. You aren't out of the woods until the examiner tells you you've passed. Just remember that."

"I will." In fact, she was pretty sure she'd have nightmares about it.

"You'll pass anyway," said Smith, making a turn that threatened to tilt them onto two wheels. "I don't think you could flip this thing over if you tried!"

"Excuse me?"

"It's so wide, you could never get the—"

"No, the other part," Melanie interrupted quickly. "About me passing the test."

"Oh, yeah. You will. Easily," Smith said, as if this weren't the biggest news of Melanie's life. "Your dad asked me to be extra tough on you, to make sure you really know your stuff, and you do. And that's not even taking into account that there isn't an examiner in that office who wouldn't be terrified to flunk a student of mine. In fact, let's go get that stupid student car and do it right now. If we hurry, we can just make it."

"Do what?" Melanie squeaked.

"Take the test. Might as well get it behind us. Why waste more time in that piece of junk when we could be driving around town in this? I'm sure your dad is going to want you to have at least a couple of lessons in your *real* car. It only makes sense. Right?"

"You're sure I'll pass," Melanie repeated. All of Smith's other words had run right past her like water.

"Slam dunk," Smith assured her. "Man, I *love* this car! Doesn't being in it just make you feel . . . powerful?"

Here goes nothing, Nicole thought nervously, trailing the rest of the cheerleading squad through the door of Victory Uniforms. They had practiced their hearts out that Thursday afternoon, showered at school, and now they were there to pick up their uniforms. Which meant they'd be trying them on first. Together.

I feel sick.

She had eaten almost no breakfast in anticipation of the dreaded event, but by lunchtime she'd been starving. Everyone had been passing around extra chips, and cookies, and those candy-coated protein bars. . . . She had easily made up for breakfast then. And that morning she had weighed exactly ten pounds more than when she'd been measured for her cheerleading skirt at the end of the previous school year.

Please, God, let it button, she prayed. *Let the zipper not blow out the second I sit down.*

"All right, people," said Sandra, holding up a hand for quiet. The ten girls completely filled the tiny front of the shop, and everyone except Nicole was talking and giggling excitedly about the new uniforms. Sandra exchanged a few words with the woman behind the counter, while Nicole distracted herself by looking around at the dusty football jerseys on the walls and the two decrepit mannequins, one in a Little League uniform and the other dressed as a somewhat faded cheerleader. The saleswoman disappeared into the back of the shop.

"This is so exciting!" Kara whispered to Nicole. "I hope they came out cute."

"They'll be cute," said Tanya, overhearing. "Melanie all but designed them herself."

She gave Nicole a look that didn't do a thing for Nicole's nerves.

She still wishes it was Melanie here instead of me, she thought. *And it should be Melanie. If she hadn't given me her space on the squad . . .*

"Here we go!" the saleswoman said loudly, reappearing with a uniform sheathed in layers of plastic. She put it down on the counter and be-gan unwrapping, eventually raising the first piece in triumph.

"Here's the sweater," she announced, turning it back and forth so that everyone could get a good look. The girls oohed and ahhed excitedly, and even Nicole felt her spirits lift. The sweater was way cuter than last year's, which Nicole would have gladly killed to possess.

"And the shell." The woman held up the braid-trimmed sleeveless top that was worn with the skirt in warm weather. "And the skirt!"

The skirt was the same green as the sweater, its short length divided into countless tiny pleats. Two gold stripes ran parallel to the hem, the jaggedness of the pleats making them look like lightning bolts. At the waistband, a single green button was all that showed of the closing—the zipper was invisible.

Please let it fit. Please let it fit, Nicole prayed over and over.

Sandra glanced at her watch. "We need to get

these tried on fast," she announced. "I have another appointment."

The squad went silent immediately.

"Whose uniform is that?" Sandra asked the saleswoman.

The woman dug through the plastic some more and eventually found a tag. "Nicole Brewster," she announced.

Nicole felt her hands go cold.

"How many dressing rooms do you have?" Sandra asked.

"Four."

The coach's mouth tugged impatiently. She asked the saleswoman to bring out the rest of the uniforms, then turned back to her squad.

"Nicole, take your uniform and go put it on. Hurry. You girls will have to double up in the dressing rooms, and even then we're two spaces short. Please don't dawdle."

No one had to tell Nicole to hurry. Grabbing her uniform, she dashed down the short hall containing the dressing rooms, locking herself into the farthest one. If she hurried, maybe she could get dressed before she had to let anyone else in. The last thing she wanted was for one of the other girls to see the roll of fat that was sure to be bulging around her waist.

As she skinned off her shorts and tank top, Nicole could hear the saleslady rummaging around in more plastic. Normally, standing in her underwear between three-way mirrors meant a chance to view and criticize herself from every angle, but Nicole barely even glanced at her reflection before grabbing the skirt. If she could just get it on, then get the sweater on over it before anyone saw, maybe that would hide her stomach. With shaking hands she stepped into the unzipped skirt, shimmying it up over her hips.

No problem there, at least. But she hadn't expected one, either. The pleats in a cheerleading skirt were designed to leave plenty of room for kicking, jumping, and tumbling. The tight part was the waist. Nicole sucked in her stomach and went for the button, which slipped through the buttonhole almost too easily. Holding her breath, still expecting the worst, she pulled up the zipper and stood staring in shock.

There was a two-inch gap between her waist and the band.

They made a mistake, she thought, daring to let out her breath. Even with normal posture, her waist rose slim and taut above a comfortably unrestricting waistband—not a bulge in sight. *Either they made my skirt too big, or this is someone else's.*

A sudden knock on the dressing room door nearly gave her a heart attack.

"Nicole?" called Kara. "Can I share with you?"

Still wearing only her bra and skirt, Nicole whipped her head around to check the three-way mirror. To her complete amazement, she just didn't see a problem. Was she getting too easy on herself? Or did she really look fine?

"Just a minute," she called back, fumbling with the latch. A second later, Kara walked in.

"Oh, cute!" she cried when she saw Nicole. "That fits you perfectly!"

"Yeah. Pretty good," Nicole mumbled, in a hurry to put on her shell just the same. She pulled it on over her head, then looked in the mirror again. The uniform couldn't have fit better if they'd sewn it for her that morning.

There had to be a mistake.

Her heart in her throat, Nicole began rummaging through the plastic her pieces had been wrapped in, wanting to double-check the name tag.

"How are you girls doing in there?" the saleslady asked over the door.

Leaving Kara changing, Nicole slipped into the hall.

"Perfect!" the woman pronounced when she saw her.

"Yes. But . . ." As much as Nicole would have loved to leave well enough alone, if there was a problem, she wanted to be the one who discovered it. She motioned for the lady to bend a little closer. "I think I might have someone else's uniform. I mean, maybe."

The woman looked at her strangely. "I read the name right off the label. Aren't you Nicole?"

"Yes. But you see, I . . . I've *grown* a little this summer," she whispered, mortified, "so I was afraid the skirt would be tighter. Which makes me think that maybe the uniforms got mixed up and one of the other girls has—"

"Is that all?" The woman smiled and laid a comforting hand on Nicole's arm. "We don't *expect* teenagers to stay the same size, dear. Of *course* you're still growing. We always build in some room for that."

"You—you do?" Nicole stammered, unable to believe her ears. "You people are geniuses!"

The saleswoman laughed. "Well, thanks. But I don't think we invented the idea."

She moved off to check the next room. Nicole hesitated a second, then burst back in on Kara.

"How does yours fit?" she asked.

Kara pulled the skirt away from her waist. "A little loose, but it's not going to fall off or anything."

"Growing room," Nicole said sagely. "They always leave a little."

"Oh. That's smart, I guess. I won't have to worry about having a slice of pizza after the games now."

And neither will I, Nicole realized, gazing at herself in the mirror. For the first time in months, she was happy with what she saw there. She looked fine. She looked better than fine—she looked good. Ten pounds wasn't the end of her world after all.

I don't even care if I lose them anymore.

The thought took her by surprise. Perhaps she was just giddy with relief that her uniform fit. But still . . .

Nope. I honestly don't care, she affirmed, turning her back on the mirror.

Maybe she really *had* grown that summer.

"*Please*, Jesse?" Brittany begged, hanging on his bedroom door after dinner. "Just ask one more time. One more time, that's all."

Sighing, Jesse looked up from the *Sports Illustrated* he'd been attempting to read on his bed. "And if I do, will you stop bugging me?"

"Yes! Definitely!" she promised quickly, letting go of the door.

"I don't mean just tonight. I mean, stop bugging. Period."

"Oh."

"I'll ask Elsa one more time," he bargained, "but whatever she says is what she says. I'm out of it after this."

Brittany's eyes held a flicker of fear, but she squared her shoulders and took a deep breath. "Deal," she agreed. "Just . . . just make sure you ask her really nicely."

"I'm asking her, and that's all," Jesse said, shoving off his bed and passing his stepsister in the doorway. "That was the deal."

"Yes, but—"

"But nothing."

He could hear her stocking feet padding nervously behind him as he walked down the stairs, but he didn't turn around. The truth was, he wasn't sure anymore that he'd be doing Brittany a favor by getting her out of Sacred Heart. At least she was safe there. He could take care of himself at school, but she was such a girl. . . .

He found Elsa on the back patio, enjoying the night-blooming jasmine. Twilight was falling, shrouding the yard in shadows, but he could see her silhouette clearly. Letting himself out the sliding glass door from the living room, Jesse walked straight to her.

"Listen," he said without preamble. "I've been thinking, and maybe you're right about keeping Brittany in private school."

Elsa lifted her head from the flowers, clearly surprised. Jesse heard Brittany groan from her hiding place behind the living room curtains.

"But the thing is," he continued, "she really doesn't want to be there. So not only are you going to have a fight on your hands all next year, she's probably not going to do that great in her classes."

Elsa's blue eyes narrowed appraisingly. "Go on."

"She's sure to be miserable and whiny. And personally, if I have to hear about that stupid jumper one more time I may commit hari-kari."

"I know what you mean," Elsa said with an ironic smile.

"So why not let her try Samuel Clemens? I'm sure

it's a fine school. And this way we can all get some peace."

Elsa nodded. "That's what I've been thinking too."

Had she just agreed with him? It seemed far too easy.

"You have?"

"Yes. You're right, Jesse. This isn't Los Angeles." She actually smiled at him, a grin between adults. "And this way we can *all* get some peace."

"Okay, then!" he exclaimed, taken by surprise. "Um, do you want me to tell her or . . ."

He trailed off, the illusion that Brittany hadn't already heard every word completely shattered by the way she'd begun squealing and dancing around the living room, her skinny, gyrating figure backlit by the entry lights.

Elsa only chuckled. "Yeah. Go tell her."

On the other side of the glass door, Brittany nearly attacked him.

"You did it! You did it!" she crowed, jumping up and down. "You're my *hero*!"

"Don't get so carried away."

But he couldn't deny it felt good to see her so happy. Elsa had probably made the right decision—and if not, Brittany could always transfer back.

"I'm going to be your *slave* from now on! Whatever you want done, you only have to ask."

"I don't actually need any—"

"I'll wash your car!" she offered.

"Not even," he warned quickly. "Don't touch my car, Bee—I'm not kidding."

"Your laundry, then. Or your bathroom," she said, determined to show her gratitude somehow. "I'll bake you cookies!"

"Cookies wouldn't be bad." If she was so intent on paying him back, who was he to argue?

"What kind do you want?" she asked eagerly. "I'll make them right now."

"Mmm . . . oatmeal," he decided.

Brittany spun around and practically sprinted toward the kitchen, her stocking feet slip-sliding everywhere like a puppy's.

"With chocolate chips in them," he yelled after her as she disappeared. "And raisins!"

"Whatever you want!" she called back sweetly.

Jesse shook his head at her antics. Not only was she crazy, but he had serious doubts as to her baking ability. Her cookies might not even be edible.

But that's not really the point, he remembered, smiling.

It just felt kind of good to have finally helped the kid out.

Twelve

"This is disgusting," said Ben, digging a finger into the little glass jar of pink bait Bernie had handed him.

"You don't have to use it," she said. "There are always worms and insects."

She was standing on the bank of the stream, wearing sneakers without socks and ancient denim cutoffs. The sunlight filtering through the leaves overhead dappled her bare legs and shoulders and played through her short brown hair. For her, Ben could almost imagine threading a live worm onto a fishhook. Almost.

"That's okay." He managed to extract a little glob, which he rolled into a ball. "But you have to admit this stuff stinks," he added, trying to spear his handiwork with a hook.

Bernie laughed and turned back toward the water, where her own hook bobbed peacefully beneath a clear plastic float. "What a baby," she teased. "Too bad your dad never designed any fishing games. Then maybe you'd have a clue."

"Hey, I can fish," Ben assured her. Dropping his clumsily baited hook, he hurried across the tufted grass to her side and dangled his line out over the creek. Unfortunately, it was muddy on the bank, and the bottoms of his sneakers had been worn slick by a summer filled with nature hikes. He lost his footing, his feet shooting forward while his head snapped back. The next thing he knew, he was lying flat on his back with his legs in the water, his butt in the mud, and a bright pink glob of bait dangling above his head from a pole pointing straight to the sky.

Bernie gasped. "Are you all right?" Dropping her own pole, she rushed to his side to make sure he was still breathing. And then she started to laugh.

"Very funny," he grumbled. Handing her his fishing pole, he managed to crab-crawl up the bank until his feet were out of the water.

"Sorry." She covered her mouth in an effort to stop her giggles. "You're not hurt, are you?"

"No. I just hate it when I do stuff like that."

"It was an accident," said Bernie. "It could have happened to anyone."

It could have, he thought unhappily. *But it always happens to me.*

Still, the fact that she didn't seem to think less of him made him feel a little better. Getting up, he waded into the stream and scrunched down into the water, washing the mud off his clothes.

"You know, they have machines for that now,"

Bernie called, giggling, from the bank. "Or maybe you don't go in for such newfangled appliances."

"I guess I'm just old-fashioned." And suddenly he didn't care about falling anymore. He waded back to shore laughing, happy just to be with her. "Why aren't you fishing?"

Bernie made a face. "No fish is going to bite in all that mud you stirred up. We'll have to wait."

"Sorry," Ben said, trying to keep from smiling. Fishing had been her idea, and despite his claims, he had no idea what he was doing. He found a boulder in the sun and sat down, wringing out the hem of his shirt to help it dry faster.

"Are you excited about tomorrow?" Bernie asked, sitting down beside him.

"You mean the wedding?" He thought a moment. "I guess. I'm mostly just excited that you're coming with me."

Bernie's smile crinkled her eyes into little half-moons. "I bought a new dress," she revealed.

"I thought you were saving for a computer!"

Bernie shook her head. "I'll never have that much money. Mostly I just wanted some school clothes that weren't hand-me-downs. Besides, how could I not get a dress for tomorrow? A wedding is the fanci-est place anyone's ever taken me."

Ben's chest swelled with pride. "What does your dress look like?"

"You think I'm going to tell *you*?" She shoved him

with one stiff arm, laughing as they rocked away from each other.

"Just give me a hint."

"Nope."

"Come on, Bernie. Tell me *something*. Anything." She tilted up her chin and gazed at him across smiling cheeks. "All I'm going to say is that it's also perfect for the Homecoming dance. I expect I'll get my money's worth out of it."

"Does that mean . . . ?" He stared at her uncertainly. Homecoming wasn't until November, but if she was serious, he was ready to commit that second. "I mean . . . are you asking?"

"Actually? I think you're supposed to ask me."

"Will you go?" he blurted out immediately. "I mean, with me? To the dance?"

She threw back her head and laughed. "All right. Since you asked so nicely."

Reaching out, he caught her in his arms, forgetting his wet clothes and mud and everything except how happy she made him.

"I can't believe I found you," he whispered.

"That *was* pretty lucky for you," she said, mischief sparkling in her brown eyes.

Ben just laughed and kissed her.

Who was he to disagree?

"Are you sure you aren't going to be bored?" Jesse asked Melanie as they sauntered up one sideline of the CCHS football field. He had an arm around her shoulders, pulling her body so close to his that they had to walk in step.

"I brought a book," she reminded him, holding it up. "Now that I have my driver's license, I thought I'd better read this."

He shook his head, amused. "As fascinating as the Hummer owner's manual must be, I'll bet you end up watching us more than you read."

"Yeah? Well, that was my plan anyway," she informed him, sticking out her tongue.

He smiled, and the way her heart flipped over almost made her suggest that they ditch football practice and drive up to the lake. Jesse was wearing his cleats—he looked ready for a good sprint. If they started running before anybody saw them . . .

"Jones!" someone hailed from across the field.

Melanie groaned. So much for that idea.

"There's Barry!" Jesse said excitedly, waving to some guys walking onto the grass from the other side. "And Gary, and Jeff, and Manuel." Tightening his arm around Melanie's shoulders, he started turning her in their direction. "Come on. I want you to meet them."

"I already know them," she protested, looking longingly back toward the parking lot. "As well as I want to, anyway."

"Just say hi," he insisted.

A minute later, they'd met up with Barry's group.

Melanie could see another, larger crowd bearing down on them from the gym, but Jesse didn't seem to notice.

"Hey, Barry!" he said. "You know my girlfriend, Melanie. Right?"

He put so much emphasis on the word *girlfriend* that Melanie had to press her lips together to keep from laughing. He was adorable.

"Yeah, sure," said Barry, leering.

"And this is Gary, and Jeff, and Manuel," Jesse told her, as if they hadn't just been through that. "Everyone, this is my girlfriend, Melanie." He put his other arm around her and squeezed possessively, his message clear for all to see.

"Maybe there's a cave you can drag me into by my hair," she whispered in his ear.

He laughed—a short, barking sound. "Maybe later," he whispered back.

"You wish!" she giggled, pushing him away.

Then the second group of players reached the field and Jesse began introducing her to them, too. "This is Melanie, my girlfriend," he said, over and over again. "My girlfriend, Melanie."

It was getting ridiculous by the time Coach Davis's whistle broke things up, but Jesse didn't seem to notice.

"See you after practice," he said, kissing her in front of the whole team. The other guys whistled and catcalled until one of Jesse's hands left her back and traveled around behind his own. Judging from the resulting snorts of laughter, Melanie could guess what position his fingers were in. "I love you," he said, not caring who heard.

"I love you too," she whispered, melting up against him.

"Let's go, Jones!" the coach shouted impatiently.

He kissed her one last time, then turned and sauntered off as if he owned the field. "Don't go anywhere," he called back to her over his shoulder.

Never, she thought, her insides still jelly.

She was on her way to the bleachers when the cheerleading squad emerged from the gym and started sprinting toward the sideline, Sandra calling the pace from behind. To Melanie's surprise, they were wearing their new uniforms, as if holding a dress rehearsal.

Knowing Sandra, she probably just wants to make sure nothing's going to rip, Melanie thought, a little wistfully. She had a lot of respect for the cheerleading coach, and it still bothered her that Sandra thought she had let the squad down. *If only I could explain why I quit . . .*

But she never had, for fear of jeopardizing Nicole's position.

The girls caught sight of her and began showing off, whooping, tumbling, and performing their most difficult jumps as they charged the last few yards to the sideline. Melanie smiled, knowing their display meant they still considered her a friend.

"What are you doing here?" Tanya asked, trotting out to the front of the squad.

Melanie nodded toward the field. "Jesse wanted me to watch him practice."

Tanya shook her head. "I can't believe you're going to be the good little girlfriend, sitting in the stands, when you could have been out here with us."

Melanie shrugged. "Maybe you'll twist an ankle and I'll have to take over for you. I *think* I could cut down your uniform enough to make it fit."

They grinned at each other, even.

"What do you think of the uniforms this year, Melanie?" Angela asked, spinning to give the full effect. "They came out good, don't you think?"

"She ought to like them," said Sandra, catching up to the group. "She designed them."

Melanie turned to face her former coach, startled that Sandra was speaking to her. Back in the spring, an angry Sandra had made it clear that they had nothing left to say to each other. Now Melanie saw a renewed spark of friendliness in the coach's brown eyes and a smile on her full lips.

"Well, I, uh . . . I wanted you guys to look good," Melanie dared to tease. "I knew you'd need all the help you could get."

"Ha ha." Sandra rolled her eyes, but they came

right back to Melanie's. They seemed to be trying to tell her something. Something important . . .

She knows! Melanie realized suddenly. How the coach had figured it out was anyone's guess, but Melanie had no doubt that Sandra had finally divined her true reason for leaving the squad. *She knows, and she isn't mad anymore!*

The relief was indescribable. It had been terrible having Sandra think badly of her, knowing she believed that Melanie was indecisive or selfish, or both.

"So, I guess we'll see you at the games," Sandra said, motioning for the squad to follow her to the benches.

"You'll see me," Melanie promised happily. "You'll *definitely* see me."

The girls moved off, Nicole lagging behind for a chance to talk.

"You should be wearing this, not me," she said uneasily, looking down at her new uniform. "Are you sorry you gave me your place?"

"Not at all." Melanie shook her head. "Not now."

"Well . . . next year, you'll be on the squad again."

Melanie smiled. "Next year, I'll be captain."

"I'm not sure spaghetti was the best choice for Jason," Jenna whispered to Peter at the rehearsal dinner Friday night.

Peter glanced to his opposite side to catch a peek

at his new little brother. Jason seemed to be wearing at least as much pasta as he had eaten. Meat sauce ran down his cheeks and chin, and the front of his white dress shirt looked like it belonged in a Quentin Tarantino film. As Peter watched, Jason used his fork to convey more strands of spaghetti to his mouth, then sucked them up with relish, their loose ends hurling sauce like a dropped garden hose with the water on full blast. If Peter had learned anything new about Jason in the past couple of days, it was that table manners weren't his strong point.

"Yeah. But look how happy he is," Peter told Jenna, smiling.

Both their families were seated around the extra-long table the staff at Angelo's had created by pushing three smaller square tables together and covering them with red-and-white tablecloths. Vases of daisies and candles in wicker-covered wine bottles clustered at the center, adding to the festive appearance. Nearly all the rest of the table was covered by china and crystal; between the antipasto salad, the bread, and the individually ordered entrees, all thirteen members of the party had at least three plates and two glasses each, and dessert hadn't even been served yet.

Jenna leaned around Peter for another look at Jason, shaking her head as the boy began capping his fingertips with olives from his salad. Mrs. Altmann whispered something to him, and the olives disappeared into Jason's mouth.

"What's it like?" Jenna asked curiously. "Sharing your mother with a whole new person?"

Peter checked to make sure Jason wasn't listening before he answered. "Honestly? It's weird . . . but it's good. I'm glad."

Jenna nodded thoughtfully. "It's just so hard to imagine. Even though I've known Jason all this time, suddenly he seems like someone completely new, because he's with you guys. It's like I never even saw him before."

Peter knew what she meant. It wasn't that Jason had changed so much, but the situation had changed drastically—and that made everything seem different. Suddenly Jason was under a microscope, and so were they, his new guardians.

I never even noticed his table manners before, thought Peter, fixing on an example. *And now it's up to us to fix them.*

Of course, that sort of stuff was mostly his parents' responsibility, but still . . . adopting Jason had been his idea.

Dear God, give me strength, he prayed impulsively. *And wisdom, and patience, and persistence, and whatever else I'll need for this. I know you only give good gifts. Thank you for the gift of Jason.*

Peter opened his eyes again, already feeling calmer. It was always a relief to remember that no matter how much he took on, he never truly worked alone.

"I'd like to propose a toast!" Mr. Conrad announced, rising at the head of the table. He held up his wineglass, tapping on it with a fork. "To Caitlin and David. May they be very happy."

Everyone held up a glass, David never taking his eyes off Caitlin. Jenna's shy sister managed to keep her chin up despite the blush on her cheeks. All through the wedding rehearsal at their church that afternoon, Caitlin's voice had barely risen above a whisper, but there was something new in the way she walked and in the way she held herself. Peter was starting to suspect that anyone who attempted to cross her on something she cared about would find her less of a pushover than they'd imagined.

"Doesn't Caitlin look happy?" Jenna sighed.

"Not as happy as David."

She grinned at him, obviously pretty happy herself. "It was weird today, standing up at the altar, looking at you. . . ." As the maid of honor and the best man, they'd been placed directly across from each other.

"Why?" he teased. "Am I that funny-looking?"

She rolled her eyes, her cheeks growing pinker. "You know what I mean."

He did, actually, but he found being her partner

there more exciting than weird. He had every hope of standing at that altar with her again someday, one position closer to Reverend Thompson.

"Wait until you see us Altmann men in our new suits tomorrow," he warned her. "You'll probably swoon or something."

Jenna burst out laughing.

"You never know." Peter did his best to look serious, but he couldn't quite pull it off.

"I'll take my chances." Flipping her long brown hair back over one shoulder, Jenna leaned in close, her blue eyes sparkling. "Tomorrow is going to be great, isn't it?"

"The best," he said, forgetting his worries. "*Everything's* going to be great."

Thirteen

Jenna stood at the altar as organ music played, swaying unsteadily on her heels. She had just walked up the aisle, her butter yellow satin dress brushing her calves with each slow step, and now she was waiting across from Peter, nervously wringing the juices from the stems of her daisy bouquet. Peter and David looked as handsome as Peter had jokingly predicted in their new navy blue suits, boutonnieres of pale yellow roses on their lapels. Peter winked at her, breaking the tension a little, and Jenna dared to turn her head and look back down the aisle.

Mary Beth was walking up to join them. As the maid of honor, Jenna might have walked last, but since Peter was the only groomsman, Caitlin had decided he should escort Jenna first and then stand beside his brother, letting the other girls follow in order of age. Mary Beth's steps were measured and ceremonious as she slowly approached the altar, but the grin on her freckled face was anything but somber. Her auburn curls were piled high on her head, and the long ribbon tails on her bouquet reached nearly to her hem, echoing the fluffy white bows on the end of every pew. Jenna saw the people sitting there, but not their faces, nervousness and excitement making their features a blur. The only faces that were clear to her were those of her mother, in the first pew on the left side, and Mr. and Mrs. Altmann, with Jason in a navy blue suit, on the right.

Mary Beth reached the altar and took her place just as Maggie started her walk up the aisle. She looked like a smaller version of Mary Beth—except for the wreath of daisies surrounding her piled curls. Maggie carried a bouquet as well, but she held her head triumphantly, showing off the flowers she'd *really* wanted.

Allison came next, and to Jenna's surprise, she had Sarah's cane tucked under one arm. A murmur ran through the pews, everyone wondering the same thing: How would Sarah reach the altar without her cane?

Then Sarah appeared, all blond hair and pale yellow satin, beaming like an angel at the end of the aisle. With slow, careful steps she made her way to the front of the church, walking without a cane for the first time since the accident that had nearly taken her life. Her gait was awkward, one foot twisted and dragging behind the other, but to Jenna's eyes it was the most beautiful thing she had ever seen. Tears of joy blurred her vision and she didn't try to hide them as she half laughed, half wept with the force of her emotion. By the time Sarah arrived at the special chair that had been placed beside Allison for her, there wasn't a dry eye in the house. Jenna didn't think she could be any happier.

And then she saw the bride. Mr. Conrad emerged at the end of the aisle with Caitlin, the organist launched into "Here Comes the Bride," and everyone in the pews rose to their feet, craning their necks to see. Caitlin glowed on her father's arm, her smile rising up from the depths of her soul. Her simple white dress looked exactly right, falling just to the floor. Her light brown hair tumbled to her shoulders, its only ornament five or six daisies pinned individually around her head, nestling in her curls. No hat, no veil, no gloves, no train . . .

She looked absolutely perfect.

Caitlin floated down the aisle on her father's arm, and by the time Reverend Thompson asked who gave the bride away and Mr. Conrad answered, "Her mother and I do," Jenna had already soaked the lace handkerchief she'd brought up hidden beneath her bouquet.

"I have extras," Mary Beth whispered, slipping Jenna a tissue. "This could be a wet ride."

Jenna took the tissue gratefully, managing to get her face mostly dry before Caitlin handed her the bride's bouquet. Caitlin's bouquet was like the others, only larger—a simple bouquet of daisies, their combined stems lined up and chopped off evenly, a wide white ribbon holding the whole together.

"Dearly beloved," Reverend Thompson began, "we are gathered together here in the sight of God, and in the face of this company, to join together this man and this woman in holy matrimony. . . ."

The familiar words rolled over Jenna. She heard them, but there were so many other things in her heart and mind that they didn't truly register until the climax.

"I, David, take thee, Caitlin, to be my wedded wife . . ." David's voice was firm but his expression was tender as he recited his vows to Caitlin.

"I, Caitlin, take thee, David, to be my wedded husband . . ." Jenna had expected her shy sister's voice to shake, speaking in front of so many people, but while Caitlin's voice was low, every word was clear. ". . . to have and to hold from this day forward; for better, for worse; for richer, for poorer; in sickness and in health; to love and to cherish, till death us do part, according to God's holy ordinance; and thereto I give thee my troth."

Then David slipped a gold ring over Caitlin's nail and down her slender finger. Caitlin reciprocated with a matching band, her hand shaking less than his. There were more words, a prayer, and the next thing Jenna knew, the reverend was pronouncing David and Caitlin man and wife.

"You may now kiss the bride," he added.

Caitlin blushed as David gave her a short, sweet kiss on the lips, but she obviously didn't mind. The newlyweds turned around and everyone applauded as they swept down the aisle. Jenna was so busy clapping that she'd have forgotten to move if Peter hadn't offered his arm.

"That was great, wasn't it?" he whispered as they walked.

Jenna tucked in tighter to his shoulder. "I may not stop crying for the rest of the day."

"You'd better," he said, smiling, "or who's going to sing in the band?"

The band! she thought with a thrill of anticipation. As much as she would have enjoyed standing on the church steps to throw birdseed at Caitlin and David, she had to hurry and change clothes in order to beat the wedding party to the Lakehouse Lodge. There she'd meet up with Guy, Paul, and Evan, to be ready to play when the newlyweds arrived.

As Jenna and Peter entered the vestibule, she gave his arm a quick squeeze good-bye, then peeled off toward the side hallway that led back to the choir room.

"See you soon," he called, engulfed by the congregation as it came tumbling out behind them.

Her pink prom dress was hanging where she'd left it, waiting to be worn for her first gig with Trinity. The guys had bought gray slacks, white shirts, and matching ties for the occasion, and Jenna had been excited about how well her pink would go with their gray. As she reached for her favorite dress now, though, she found herself unexpectedly reluctant to take off the yellow satin Caitlin had chosen.

After all, I am the maid of honor. And nobody really cares if I match the guys.

She stood there, hesitating.

And all of a sudden she realized that she *liked* the yellow dress. Despite her plans and pleas for a wedding that was more sophisticated and formal, now that she'd seen it, she couldn't find fault with a single thing Caitlin had chosen. The whole ceremony had been so sweet, so right, so perfectly Caitlin. . . .

Grabbing her lace shawl off the hanger, Jenna abandoned her prom dress and ran for the Conrads' station wagon. She had a feeling she was never going to feel the same negative way about yellow again.

"I can't believe how beautiful this place is in daylight," Leah told Miguel.

"I thought it looked pretty good in the dark. I remember *something* looked good at the prom," he teased.

They had arrived early at the wedding reception and wandered outside to check the view from the wooden deck that wrapped around the back of the hotel and extended over the water. Leah shaded her eyes against the sunlight bouncing back from the calm green ripples of a perfect summer day. Beyond the lake, the hills were bathed in light. And when Leah turned to look back at the lodge, she could see arriving wedding guests through the reception room's tall windows, milling about, talking, and admiring the pale yellow three-tiered wedding cake on a special table at the end of the buffet. As Leah watched, Jenna and the other members of Trinity stepped onto the dais at one end of the room and began rechecking the instruments and microphones they had set up earlier.

"Look, it's starting," Leah said excitedly, towing Miguel back inside to the party. The band began playing some background music while the growing crowd waited for the bride and groom to show. Leah spotted Ben and Bernie in a corner with glasses of lemonade, oblivious to the world around them. Ben actually looked kind of dapper in his suit, and Bernie wore her pale blue dress like Cinderella at the ball. Then Melanie and Jesse walked in from the parking lot, holding hands as if ready to star in their own romantic movie, and Leah shook her head, amazed by the change in them both.

"You know, things worked out pretty well," she said, snuggling into Miguel's arms. "None of us was in a relationship when we formed Eight Prime, and now everyone's in love."

"Aren't you forgetting someone?" Miguel nodded toward the doorway.

Nicole had just walked in—alone. She was wearing a summery print with very high heels and too much eyeliner, but something about her manner made her seem like a lost little girl. She glanced around the room, let her eyes hesitate on the band, then headed directly for Leah and Miguel.

"Can I hang out with you guys?" she asked. "I feel pretty conspicuous standing around on my own."

"Sure," Leah said sympathetically. Still, as far as she was concerned, showing up alone was better than showing up with that buffoon Noel. There were worse things than being single. She was about to suggest that they all get some lemonade when a drumroll heralded the arrival of the wedding party.

The bridesmaids came in first, then Peter, holding Jason firmly by one hand. The parents of the bride and groom followed, and finally Caitlin and David themselves, greeted by cheers from the guests.

"Ladies and gentlemen," Guy said at the microphone. "It is my honor to introduce—for the first time ever—Mr. and Mrs. David Altmann!"

Leah felt herself getting choked up as the crowd applauded. *What would it be like*, she wondered, *to be introduced as someone's wife?*

She turned to Miguel, but his eyes were on the newlyweds, who had begun circulating through the room, exchanging handshakes and kisses. The band broke into a lively song, and everyone started talking excitedly. The reception was officially underway.

Waiters began coming around with trays filled

with hors d'oeuvres, and flutes of champagne and sparkling water. Leah accepted a glass of water, admiring the wafer-thin slice of lemon on its rim. "This is nice," she said, looking around the room.

"Yes," Nicole agreed wistfully.

Then Jenna took the microphone. "May I have everyone's attention?" she asked above the chatter. She looked nervous in her yellow dress, her weight shifting back and forth on dyed-to-match shoes.

"Caitlin . . . David . . . ," she said as the voices quieted down. "I wrote this song for you. It's your wedding present."

A surprised murmur filled the room as the band began to play. Even the Conrads seemed taken unawares. The crowd split to let Caitlin and David up to the stage, and then Jenna started to sing:

"Now and always,
Love is patient, love is kind.
It always protects, always trusts, always perseveres.
Now and always,
If I sing like an angel but have not love,
I am nothing.
Love does not envy, it does not boast,
It is not proud.
Love rejoices with the truth.
Love never fails.
On this, your wedding day,

May Love be with you,
Now and always."

Jenna's voice was so beautiful that Leah's skin broke into goose bumps, and the torrent of applause when she finished went on and on. Jenna took a few blushing curtsies, clearly both surprised and pleased by the warmth of the crowd's reaction. Then she stepped off the edge of the stage to hug the bride and groom.

"Ugh," groaned Nicole, letting her head roll back. "Now I *really* feel bad."

Leah wrapped a comforting arm around her friend's shoulders.

"I'd say Trinity just launched their wedding career with a bang," Miguel predicted. "That song may have been written for Caitlin, but it's going to get played at every wedding in town."

"It *was* really pretty," Leah said, trying to remember exactly where the lyrics had come from. Jenna had changed things around, but Leah recognized the source as a Bible passage.

Guy took the microphone again. "Caitlin and David have asked everyone to help themselves to lunch," he said, gesturing toward the tables where waiters in white coats had begun removing the lids from the buffet. "Sit wherever you like, and enjoy the day. And the music. We're Trinity."

The band launched into another song, and Leah smiled. "Their music is good. They could use more work on their patter."

"They'll get it," said Miguel.

Nicole wiped her wet eyes with a tissue, removing half her makeup. "Are we going to eat or what?"

The three of them got in line, piling freshly baked rolls with the smoked turkey and roast beef being carved to order by chefs in tall hats. There were so many delicious-looking side dishes that Miguel ended up with two full plates, and even Nicole's was loaded.

"Pick a table. Hurry," said Miguel, juggling his food.

Leah found one near the edge of the dance floor. They had barely sat down when Ben, Bernie, Melanie, and Jesse all joined them. The tables were set for eight, which left Nicole with an empty space next to her. Leah looked around for Peter, but he was sitting with the wedding party. Once again she felt a pang of sympathy for Nicole.

It must be even harder to be the third wheel when your ex is in the room, Leah thought.

Nicole hadn't so much as mentioned Guy's presence, but Leah couldn't help noticing the way her eyes kept drifting to the band.

"They're awesome, aren't they?" said Ben, following Nicole's gaze. "I'm glad we got to hear them."

Melanie was trying to spread mustard with a carrot stick. "Me too. Jenna must be so excited."

"Where's your knife?" Jesse asked, noticing what she was doing. "Here. Take mine."

Bernie leaned forward, her eyes darting around as if she were about to impart a major secret. "The cake has lemon filling," she revealed. "A waiter told me. That's why it's yellow."

"I just hope it tastes as good as it looks," Ben said. "When are they going to open the presents?"

The six members of Eight Prime not related to the bride and groom had chipped in on two settings of Caitlin's china. Leah had placed the gift-wrapped boxes on the designated table when she'd come in.

"They'll probably do that later, after everyone leaves," she said. "We'll get a thank-you note."

"Oh," said Ben, disappointed.

Lunch went on for another hour, guests milling about to talk to friends at other tables or pile their plates with seconds. Leah spotted Chris Hobart and his girlfriend, Maura, at a table on the other side of the dance floor and pointed them out to Miguel. Chris had helped Peter start the Junior Explorers, but no one had seen much of him that summer.

At last the toasts began, followed by the tossing of the garter. Caitlin wasn't about to have any article of her clothing removed in public, but she'd brought a spare for David to throw. Ben ran out eagerly to join the single men on the dance floor, but Miguel and Jesse both had to be pushed. One of David's friends snagged the prize, waving it over his head like a miniature lasso.

No one had to coax the girls onto the floor for a chance to catch Caitlin's bouquet. They jostled and giggled, and when the beribboned bunch of daisies arced above their heads, Leah found herself reaching for it with true desire. It cleared her outstretched fingers, though, hitting Maura Kennedy squarely in the chest. For a moment, the flowers seemed to stick there by themselves. Then Maura closed her arms, trapping the bouquet, and everybody clapped.

"Ooh, Chris!" Peter teased, yelling across the floor. "Is there something you're not telling us?"

Maura laughed as her boyfriend jumped up to join her.

"As a matter of fact, there is," Chris said. "We weren't planning to announce this today, but . . . we're getting married next Christmas!"

Everyone cheered. Peter bounded over to congratulate his friends. And as the applause died down, David signaled to the band.

"It's time for the first dance!" Guy announced excitedly. "Dancing together for the very first time . . . Mr. and Mrs. David Altmann!"

David led Caitlin out onto the floor, where they made slow circles to the music, Caitlin's long skirt just skimming the boards.

"How romantic," Melanie sighed. "Don't they make the perfect couple?"

Soon the rest of the wedding party started pairing off on the dance floor, motioning for the guests to come join them. Caitlin and David were quickly boxed in on all sides, surrounded like the pearl in an oyster.

"Do you want to dance?" Miguel asked Leah.

She had never wanted to more. She held his hand tight as he led her out, and the moment her feet touched wood her body flowed up against his. The other people in the room faded away as Leah danced with Miguel, her cheek against his shoulder. To be in his arms felt so right, she knew it was where she belonged.

Now and always.

She held him closer and tried not to think, but her mind just wouldn't be still.

Will we ever dance at our own wedding?

Don't be such a baby! Just do it! Nicole chastised herself. She had waited hours to talk to Guy, and now that the band was taking a break, she finally had a chance.

Too bad I've completely lost my nerve.

A room full of so many couples, all so clearly in love with each other, was obviously not the best place to try to start a conversation with an ex-boyfriend. On the other hand, it was the only place she was likely to get the opportunity. Nicole gripped her glass of lemonade harder and sidled up to the table where Guy was finishing a quick, belated lunch with the band.

"Hi, Nicole!" said Jenna, saving her the awkwardness of having to break in on their conversation. "Are you having a good time?"

"Really good," Nicole lied, nodding too fast and far too long. She tried to stop herself, but her neck had developed a mind of its own.

"Are you sure?" Jenna pressed. "I haven't seen you dancing."

Nicole must not have succeeded in hiding her wince, because Jenna suddenly seemed to see her mistake.

"I mean, I guess you've been too busy talking to all your friends," she added hurriedly. "You know what? I think they're about to cut the cake. Come on, Paul, Evan. Let's go get some."

Jenna practically hauled her fellow band members to their feet, hustling them off so that Nicole could be alone with Guy. What the approach lacked in subtlety it made up for in efficiency, and Nicole was grateful despite her embarrassment.

"So, uh, how've you been?" she asked, fumbling her way into the chair Jenna had just vacated. Dirty plates littered the tablecloth and she pushed one away, making room to set down her drink. "Long time, no see."

Inside her head she was dying. *Long time, no see?* she thought with a silent groan. *There's an original line!*

"Yeah."

Guy turned his gaze to meet hers, and every muscle in her body froze. After all the time she'd known him, all of a sudden he looked so good to her she could barely breathe. His reddish brown hair fell over the same intelligent blue eyes. His nose was just as curved. Physically he was no heartbreaker. But Nicole's was breaking now. For the first time in her life, she was seeing a boy as more than the sum of his features.

Why did I ever break up with him? Gail was right—I am an idiot. She hadn't come to Guy's table with the idea of getting back together, but suddenly that was all she could think about. *Should I apologize? Like he cares!*

"So what did you think of the band?" he asked.

"Oh, great! Fantastic!"

The look on his face seemed skeptical, as if she had overdone it. "I thought 'Now and Always' went over pretty well."

"Everyone loved that!" she exclaimed. "Did you help Jenna write it?"

"Jenna did the lyrics, and the rest of us helped with the music. Not that she didn't have her own ideas. We must have changed that tune fifty times."

"I thought so!" Nicole said triumphantly. "Right

after the first 'now and always,' in the 'love is patient' part. I thought the harmonies there were all different."

Guy's eyebrows went up.

"What?" she asked nervously.

"When did you hear the song before?"

Her stomach dropped as she realized her mistake. She had heard it eavesdropping outside his garage— not something she cared to explain.

"Well, you know. Jenna sang it to me." She waved a dismissive hand, almost knocking over her lemonade.

"She sang it to you in *harmony*?"

He had her. Especially since he could always ask Jenna later. It was embarrassing to be caught in such a stupid mistake, but in the grand scheme of screw-ups where Guy was concerned, this one seemed pretty minor.

"All right," Nicole admitted. "I drove by your house one night when you guys were practicing and I kind of . . . listened."

"You listened while you were driving by?"

Nicole sighed. "I *parked* and listened, all right?"

"Why?"

"I just . . ."

A list of excuses ran through her mind: She was in the area; she was curious to hear how the band sounded with the addition of Jenna; she had taken a wrong turn and stumbled upon his house by accident.

"I just . . . kind of missed you," she conceded at last.

Guy rocked back in his chair, a disbelieving smile on his lips. "There's something I never expected to hear you say."

"Well . . . people change." She dropped her eyes to the tablecloth, pushing a bread crumb around with her fingernail.

"Do they? I hope so."

Her eyes snapped back up to his. Whatever he had meant by that, the way he'd said it sounded more encouraging than she had any right to expect.

"I've changed a lot this summer," she told him.

He shrugged. "I'll bet we've both grown up some."

"Probably."

They smiled cautiously at each other. Something had been settled between them, although Nicole still wasn't sure what. She was trying to think of a way to find out when a rim shot off Paul's drum turned Guy's attention to the stage. Jenna and Evan were up there as well, Evan strapping on his bass.

"Oops. I have to go," Guy said, jumping to his feet. "They're going to start playing without me."

"I thought you were the leader of the band," she countered, trying to keep him with her a little longer.

"That's a good one," he said with a laugh. "I have to go. I'll see you, Nicole."

He ran off toward the dais, leaving Nicole wondering what he had meant. "See you" didn't have to mean anything.

But it could, she thought hopefully.

She watched as Guy took his microphone and began singing a popular song. In her mind she was back at the Hearts for God rally in L.A., watching him perform a Christian song for a crowd of screaming girls. She hadn't been completely sure what they'd seen in him at the time. Now she knew.

They saw his heart.

Nicole took a deep breath and made a vow, feeling it all the way down to her soul.

If I do get a second chance with Guy, next time I won't blow it.

Fourteen

"This place is packed!" Melanie exclaimed as they walked in, shouting to Jesse over the blaring jukebox, the din of arcade games, and the voices of the standing-room-only crowd. Noise bounced around the dim, barnlike interior of The Danger Zone until it was hard to tell which sounds were coming from the games stationed around the perimeter of the giant room and which from the army of picnic tables and benches cramming its center. A few heroic waitresses wove bravely through the oblivious crowd, the Zone's trademark greasy pizzas and pitchers of soda held high above their heads.

"Peter said he'd try to save a table," Jesse shouted back, standing on his toes to see better.

"You're never going to find him like that. We're going to have to walk around." Grabbing her boyfriend's hand, Melanie pulled him into the fray.

When the members of Eight Prime had decided at Caitlin's wedding to meet up later at The Danger Zone, they had known it might be crowded. For one thing, the combination restaurant/arcade was a popular Saturday-night hangout. More importantly, that Saturday night was the final one of the CCHS summer.

"I see Jenna," Jesse said, towing Melanie off in a different direction.

Melanie looked ahead and spotted Jenna dancing on a bench, her long brown hair snaking across her back.

"Whoa, Jenna's cutting loose!"

"She's a rock star now," Jesse reminded her, laughing.

A moment later, Leah jumped up to join Jenna, the two of them laughing and holding on to each other, barely keeping their balance. All of Eight Prime seemed to be running on adrenaline that night, cranked up by the wedding and the impending start of the new school year. Everyone at the table stood up to greet Melanie and Jesse.

"Hi! Hi!" Melanie said as she and Jesse crammed in next to Ben and Bernie. Nicole and Courtney Bell were directly across from her at the table, along with Nicole's cousin, Gail. Miguel and Peter were at the other end of Nicole's bench; Leah and Jenna were still attempting to dance on the other end of Melanie's.

"Did you guys order yet?" Jesse asked loudly.

Nicole nodded. "We got enough pizza for everyone, but they still haven't even brought our drinks."

"The waitresses look a little busy," said Jenna, jumping off the bench.

Leah got down too and the pair of them sat across from Peter and Miguel. The waitress showed up with pitchers of soda and glass mugs a moment later, miraculously managing to balance everything on a tray.

"I'll bring your third pitcher in a minute," she said, glancing over her shoulder at the dangerous path she'd just walked. "Truth is, I wasn't feeling that lucky."

She disappeared into the crowd, and Peter began pouring root beer for everyone.

"We should have a toast," Melanie proposed.

Nicole groaned. "We've been toasting things all day."

"True. But we haven't toasted ourselves—and I think we deserve it. To us!" she said, holding her glass aloft. "To Eight Prime, and the end of a fantastic year together, and the start of a fantastic year ahead."

Everyone raised their glasses, even Courtney, Bernie, and Gail. Root beer sloshed and glasses clinked all around the table.

And all of a sudden Melanie realized something amazing: She was happy. Happier even than before her mother died.

Looking around, her eyes nearly filled with tears as she realized how many friends she had. And these were *real* friends, the kind who'd go to the bottom with her—and had—not the old group of hangers-on who had cared primarily about riding her reputation. Tanya and Angela had been the only genuine friends among them, and in gaining Eight Prime she hadn't lost them. In fact, they were probably in the room somewhere too.

"You know what? It *is* going to be a good year," she whispered to Jesse.

How could it be bad? Her father was working again, she had a new car and her driver's license, she was in love . . .

Squeezing her eyes shut, she sent a quick thought up to her mother. *Don't think I don't still care, or that I don't still miss you, but . . . I just feel like things will be okay now. I know you'd want me to be happy.*

When her eyes opened again, Jesse's face was an inch from hers. "Whatcha thinking about?" he asked.

"Everything. This. Us. Next year."

He leaned in closer and she knew he was going to kiss her, right in front of all those people. "Next year is going to be great," he promised.

And even before his lips touched hers, she knew that he was right.

"So, what do people wear on the first day at this school of yours?" Gail asked Nicole. They were crossing the street with Courtney, having decided to leave the mob scene in The Danger Zone long enough to get a frozen yogurt.

"I don't know," Nicole said distractedly, her

194

attention on the passing headlights. "What do they wear at yours?"

"That's what I'm asking you."

Nicole thought her cousin was being intentionally difficult again. For the past few days, ever since their joint crying jag in the mall, they'd been getting along much better, but Gail hadn't reformed overnight. The occasional annoying comment was still very much part of her repertoire.

"You're asking *me* what people wear at *your* school," Nicole said irritably as they reached the sidewalk. From her new vantage point she could see that the frozen yogurt shop was doing nearly as much business as The Danger Zone. The line of customers stretched out the door and around the corner.

"Right. Because it's exactly the same as what they'll be wearing at yours."

Courtney got it first. She stopped dead on the sidewalk halfway to the end of the line. "You mean . . . are you . . . are you *transferring?*" she asked, her green eyes going round.

Gail nodded, and a moment later all three of them were jumping up and down, hugging and squealing like maniacs.

"What? But . . . how?" Nicole got out between hops.

Gail broke the circle and took a step backward, giving herself room to explain. "Brace yourselves, but my parents have decided that Nicole is such a good influence on me that they want to keep us together for senior year."

Nicole was speechless. Courtney, on the other hand, started laughing so hard she bent double. Her delighted peals filled the warm night air, causing heads to turn their way.

"I know!" Gail said. "Hilarious! I'd have died laughing myself if I wasn't so happy just to get out of Mapleton. There's nothing for me there."

"But . . . but . . . how are you going to register when you don't even live in Clearwater Crossing?" Nicole didn't think the idea of her being a good influence was *quite* as funny as Courtney did, but she was having a hard time grasping it too.

"I don't, but you do," Gail replied, looking mighty pleased with herself. "I'm going to use your address until my parents find a house to rent in Clearwater Crossing. By the way, I'll probably be sleeping over a lot."

Uh-oh, thought Nicole. "Do my parents know about this?"

"Of course. Your mom's thrilled that my mom's going to be around to help with the baby, and my mom's delirious to be getting me away from my old crowd. Good for my sketchy psyche and all that— not to mention my reputation."

"But your house . . . ," Nicole began.

"My dad's going to rent it out, so if they want to they can always move back after I graduate. Let me tell you, the adults all think they're geniuses for cooking up this plan." Gail smiled, and this time the roguishness of her grin was infectious. "Which is exactly what I wanted them to think."

Courtney had finally managed to stop laughing. "This is great! We'll do everything together. We'll be like the Three Musketeers!"

Gail laughed. "Or the Three Stooges."

"Charlie's Angels," Courtney countered.

"We'll be totally inseparable!" Nicole broke in, her excitement growing by the second. "This'll be the most awesome senior year anyone ever had!"

"That's the idea, cuz." Gail looped one arm around Nicole's waist and the other around Courtney's and started steering them to the back of the yogurt line.

"I'm actually getting excited about school now," Courtney said. "Three really *is* a prime number," she added for Nicole's benefit.

"Yeah. *Or*," said Nicole, thinking quickly, "*or* if the rest of Eight Prime wants to stay together after Leah and Miguel leave, Gail could join us and we'd have seven. Seven's a prime number too. Unless you join, Court. Then we'd be back up to eight."

"Me in the God Squad?" Courtney rolled her eyes. "I don't think so."

"Okay. Well . . . hey, I'll bet Bernie will want to join!" Nicole realized. "We *will* have eight again."

"Not so fast!" Courtney protested. "I didn't say I *wouldn't*."

197

They reached the end of the long line, their arms still around each other.

"We're going to have so much fun," Nicole said dreamily.

She didn't care about the fiasco with Noel anymore, or what anyone else thought of her mother having a baby, or even about her weight. She had her friends, she had her family, and maybe—if she played her cards right—she had another chance with Guy. At the very least, they were going to be friends. Suddenly she couldn't even remember why she'd been so down the past few weeks.

So I made a few mistakes. Well . . . all right, a lot of them. Isn't that how people learn?

She wasn't perfect, but she was trying. She'd come a long way in the past year. And with her friends in Eight Prime still there to support her . . .

"Next year is going to be great!" she exclaimed.

Fifteen

"Gee, Dad, do you still remember how to get there?" Jesse teased as Dr. Jones pulled his silver Mercedes out of the driveway. Elsa was in the passenger seat; Brittany sat beside Jesse in back.

"Very funny," said his father. "It's not like I've been keeping any of you from going."

Even so, no one in the Jones family had been to church since Easter, so the fact that they were all dressed up and on their way that Sunday morning seemed like a pretty big deal.

"This is a special day," Elsa said, twisting around to face her daughter. "You can't expect me to put my only child in public school tomorrow without praying for her safety."

"Ha ha," Brittany responded. "I'm not going to die, Mom."

"If you say so."

But Elsa couldn't quite hide the smile on her lips as she turned back to the front. She was actually having some fun, which wasn't like Elsa at all.

"After church, you can take us all out to brunch," Mrs. Jones informed her husband.

"Oh boy," he said, feigning disappointment. "I would . . . but I know Jesse is itching to get started on that lawn. We'd better come straight home."

"No way!" Jesse said, sitting forward on the leather seat. "I am *not* mowing that stupid lawn today. Not on the last day of summer!"

There was a split-second pause before Brittany sighed. "I'll do it," she offered heroically.

Jesse turned to stare at her, shocked. Then they all started laughing.

"What?" she demanded indignantly. "How hard can it be?"

"That big power mower would drag you around like a rag doll, Bee."

"Anyway, I was just pulling your brother's leg," Dr. Jones told her. "The lawn can skip a week."

Or you could do it, for once, Jesse thought, knowing that would never happen. His father had been spending less time barricaded in his study lately, but chores were still for other people.

"Or who knows? Maybe I'll do it," said Dr. Jones, nearly knocking Jesse off his seat. "Might be a nice change of pace."

"Yeah, Dad. It's great! You might like it so much you'll want to do it *every* week."

"Don't press your luck." But Dr. Jones smiled into the rearview mirror.

They were all in a good mood that morning.

And why not? Jesse thought suddenly. It was hard to say exactly what, but something was changing in his family. Finally, after all the fighting and hurt feelings, they were actually becoming a team. *About time, too,* he thought, relaxing back into the seat.

"I'll make you some cookies instead of cutting the lawn," Brittany promised, still suffering from hero worship. "I'll do it as soon as we get home."

"No more cookies!" Jesse groaned. She'd been baking a batch a day ever since he'd convinced Elsa to agree to Samuel Clemens. "The way you're turning those things out, you're going to get me kicked off varsity. I can't run for a touchdown with my gut dragging on the ground."

Brittany giggled. "I just want to do something nice for you."

"You already did. You've done enough."

"Really?" She seemed unconvinced.

"Listen, why don't you go meet that new friend of yours at the mall? Maybe you could get some nail polish or something for tomorrow."

Brittany's eyes widened. The students at Sacred Heart weren't allowed to wear colored polish.

"If you want, I can drop you off on my way to Melanie's," he offered.

"I'm going to Samuel Clemens Junior High School tomorrow," Brittany said with amazement, as if she had just found out.

"I know. Pretty big stuff, huh?"

Brittany just grinned at him until he couldn't help grinning back.

Leah stood with a pair of jeans in each hand, her eyes so full of tears that she could barely even see them. Every spare suitcase her family owned had been piled into her bedroom, and she wanted to hurry and fill them so she could spend her last precious hours in Clearwater Crossing with Miguel. No matter how she tried, though, she couldn't seem to concentrate enough to finish the task. The thought that she and her mother would load up the Cabrio and take off for California the next morning, as unreal as it was, had monopolized her consciousness to the point where she couldn't focus on anything else.

She wiped her tears away with the backs of her hands and gave up on trying to choose between the pants, randomly dropping one pair into an open suitcase on her bed and tossing the other to the floor.

It's not the end of the world, she told herself. *If it turns out you need something you didn't bring, you can always ask Mom to mail it to you.*

But it felt like the end of the world.

And no one could mail her Miguel.

Leah grabbed shirts blindly from her closet and threw them in on top of the jeans, mashing rather than folding. Her sweaters and other clothes were already packed. Her shoes had their own bag. If she could just finish with her closet . . .

An abrupt knock on her door sent her scurrying for a tissue. After all the sacrifices her parents had made to send her to Stanford, the last thing she wanted was for them to see her crying about going.

"Leah?" her mother called. "Can I come in?"

"Yes. Come on in," she said, taking one last sniff.

The door opened, admitting Mrs. Rosenthal and, to Leah's surprise, Miguel.

"Look who I found," her mother said, smiling. "How's the packing coming?"

"Fine," Leah lied, not even glancing at her suitcase. All she could see was her boyfriend.

Her mother seemed to understand. "I'll leave you two alone," she said, backing out and closing the door.

"What are you doing here?" Leah asked, rushing into his arms. "Is mass already over?"

"Yep. I thought you'd be done packing by now."

"Me too," she said into his shoulder. "It's just harder than I thought."

"Maybe I can help you. Hand me things, and I'll stack them in the suitcase." He twisted his body slightly, reaching past her to lift out a crumpled blouse. "Maybe even fold them," he teased.

She shook her head, her face still buried in his shirt. "That's not what's hard about it."

"Well, it seems to have eluded you so far." He pushed her gently back onto her feet. "Come on, cheer up," he urged. "Let's get this done so we can get out of here."

She nodded, but didn't move. Packing just seemed so overwhelming. Every square inch of her bed was covered with suitcases or items waiting to go in them, and she'd stacked or thrown so many other things on the floor that she could barely walk around. It felt like she'd never finish.

Part of her didn't even want to.

"Or how about we go get lunch somewhere, and then come back and tackle this?" he said. "Maybe you need a break."

She accepted eagerly. Maybe she *did* need a break. All she knew was that the sight of so many suitcases was turning her brain to mush. She told her parents where she was going, promised to be back early, and she and Miguel made their escape.

Outside, Leah felt like she could almost breathe again. The sky was a gorgeous purple-blue; the trees whispered in the breeze. She filled her lungs and didn't exhale, trying to trap summer inside her.

They decided to take her car so they could drive with the top down. The streets were quiet at that in-between hour—too late for church, too early for anything else. Leah relaxed a fraction as she drove through the tree-lined lanes, not even sure where she was headed.

"Where do you want to eat?" she asked Miguel.

"What do you feel like? Hamburgers? Or we could still get breakfast. How about pancakes?"

"I'm not even hungry," she admitted. "I just wanted to get out of my room."

"We could drive up to the lake."

She nodded, turning her car in that direction without another word. She wanted to see the lake once more before she left. Not the Lakehouse Lodge side, where the wedding had been held the day before, but the camp side, where she'd spent all summer. It was a pilgrimage, she realized as she drove, a trip she had to make to say good-bye. By the time she pulled into the parking lot, dust and gravel spitting from under her tires, she had settled into a fatalistic calm. Everything she did from this point on would be the last thing, the last time. . . .

"Come on," said Miguel, jumping out of the car and trotting around to her side. "Let's go out on our rock."

"We'll get wet," she said dubiously. The long flat rock that jutted into the lake from the shore near the parking lot was a favorite platform for summer swimmers. Even from the lot she could see a group of younger kids splashing around it.

"We'll dry."

Taking her hand, Miguel began pulling her down the long, gentle slope to the water. Leah didn't resist. Her bare feet skimmed over grass, then sand, finally reaching the mud, which squished between her toes.

Miguel had kicked off his shoes too. Now he stooped to roll up his pants before leading her through ankle-deep water, parallel to the shore.

The lake was warm in the shallows. Bits of moss floated past their feet, and sunlight reflected off the silver backs of darting minnows. By the time they reached the rock and climbed up onto its spine, the sun had heated Leah's dark hair and was tingling against her bare shoulders.

"Do you remember the first time we ever came here?" Miguel asked, leading her out to the tip of the rock. The lake surrounded them there as though they were on an island.

"Yes." They had barely known each other then, but that hadn't lasted long. "You kissed me."

The smile on his lips shone in his brown eyes. "You kissed me first."

"If you want to get all junior-high about it." Leah tried to keep a straight face but couldn't. She *had* kissed him first, and she'd never regretted it for a minute.

"I want to ask you something," he said, pulling her down to sit beside him. The rock was hot, but the place he had chosen had the advantage of being dry. For the moment, the swimmers had moved elsewhere.

"What?"

"I was wondering . . ." He shook his head. "I don't really even know how to ask this."

"What?" she said again, a little apprehensively.

He took a small blue velvet box from his pocket and Leah's heart nearly stopped.

"Is that what I think it is?" she whispered.

"Probably not," he said ruefully. "It's not an engagement ring."

He flipped the box open so she could see. A single oval sapphire gleamed at the top of a narrow gold band, tiny matching diamonds sparkling on either side. "It's a promise ring," he said. And then he found his smile again. "Leah, will you be engaged to be engaged to me?"

"Yes!" she said without hesitation, throwing her arms around his neck. "Oh, Miguel. I love you so much!"

"I love you too." He kissed the top of her head, his arms closing tightly around her. They held onto each other like that until he finally tilted his head back to see her face. "Don't you want to put it on?"

Both their hands trembled as he pushed the ring up her finger.

"Are you sure you want to do this?" she asked shakily. "I mean, everyone says long-distance relationships are so hard."

"So what. I can last as long as you can."

Leah chuckled. "You underestimate my stubbornness."

Miguel shook his head and folded her into his

arms. "I've been with you almost a year now. I don't underestimate anything."

It was true; if anyone knew her, he did. With all her heart she believed they were made for each other. They'd find a way to stay together . . . somehow. . . .

Just don't look back, she told herself, holding on for all she was worth. Straightening her left arm behind his head, she watched the reassuring flash of her ring in the sun. *We're going to make it somehow, and things will be even better than they are today.*

Don't look back. Look forward.

"Jenna!" Sarah yelled from the front door. "Peter's here."

"I'm in the kitchen!" Jenna shouted back.

Technically, it should have been Caitlin's night to do the dishes, but with Cat having left the day before, followed by Mary Beth that morning, the chore schedule needed revision. As the oldest remaining sister, Jenna had offered to pick up the slack that evening, reveling in her new position.

"Dishes, huh?" said Peter, appearing around a corner

"I'm almost done," she replied, flicking a glob of soap suds at him.

He saw it coming and ducked. "Ha! You missed for once."

She shot again and triumphed, nailing him on

one cheek. The suds slid slowly down to his jaw as he reached for a dishtowel to wipe them off. "I had to say something," he grumbled.

"Since you've already got the towel, how about drying?"

He looked at her suspiciously. "I think that was your plan all along."

She laughed and handed him a wet casserole dish. A girl didn't grow up among five sisters without learning a few good tricks.

"What's Jason doing tonight?" she asked as they worked.

"He and my mom are loading up his backpack for tomorrow, and then he's supposed to go to bed early, to rest for the first day of school." Peter smiled and rolled his eyes skyward. "I wish her luck with that one."

"He was so cute at the wedding." Jenna handed Peter another dish. "Running around in his new suit like a little gentleman."

"Yeah. The whole wedding was pretty cool."

"It was," she said, remembering. "I didn't think I'd cry, but seeing Sarah without her cane got me bawling, and after that it was all downhill."

"It's weird to have them gone. Caitlin and David, I mean."

She nodded as she rinsed the final dish. The frantic activity leading up to the wedding had started to seem like normal life—and in one day it had all just stopped. The room of her own she had wanted for so long had become a reality overnight. Two sisters had left in two days. . . .

Things were definitely different.

She dried her hands on Peter's towel and tossed it onto the counter. "Let's go out back," she said.

On the backyard porch, they rocked side by side in the large wooden swing. Fireflies flitted through the darkness, rising up out of the grass.

"So," said Peter. "Tomorrow we're seniors."

"It doesn't seem possible. Weren't we just here, starting junior year?"

He reached across and took her hand. "Yes. But we weren't *here*," he said, giving it a squeeze.

She smiled, knowing what he meant. They hadn't been a couple then. So many things had changed. She wriggled closer to him in the swing, turning her lips up to his. He was just about to kiss her when the screen door slammed like a bomb going off and Maggie ran out to interrupt them.

"What do you think of this?" she asked, twirling barefoot on the porch in a new pair of jeans and a matching cropped jacket. "Too much? Not enough?"

Jenna sighed heavily and inched away from Peter.

"For what?" he asked patiently.

"For my first day of high school!" Maggie did a few more pirouettes, so goofy with excitement that Jenna finally smiled.

"Don't worry, Maggie," she teased. "No one's going to be looking at a lowly freshman anyway."

"Hey!" her sister protested.

"You might as well get used to it," Peter told her, playing along. "Jenna and I, well . . . seniors are the *royalty* of high school. Freshmen are more like the serfs."

"*Hey!*" Maggie repeated, outraged. Peter and Jenna both burst out laughing.

"We're kidding," Peter told her.

"But only a little," Jenna couldn't resist adding.

Maggie rolled her eyes. "What about my outfit?"

"Does it matter what I say?" Jenna asked. "You'll change it anyway."

"You think I should change?" She was gone before Jenna could stop her, spilling over with nervous energy.

"I'm glad I'm not a freshman," Jenna said, remembering her first day of high school. "That first week is a little nerve-racking."

"First week? More like the whole first year." Peter pushed his feet against the porch, setting their swing rocking. "Being a senior is definitely the way to go. Just think of everything we'll get to do this year."

"Nicole called me a couple of hours ago. She wants to keep Eight Prime together. Maybe add new people. Maybe make it even bigger."

Peter nodded thoughtfully. "Melanie wants to

help me with Junior Explorers, now that Chris is out."

"I'll help you too," Jenna said, reaching for his hand again.

"Maybe we can do some more fund-raisers. If enough people are into it."

"What would we raise money for?"

He shook his head, smiling. "I don't know. We still have to maintain the bus, but aside from that the Junior Explorers are in pretty good shape now. It might be time for a new project."

"A new project?" she said excitedly. "How fun! What should it be?"

He shrugged. "We'll just have to wait and see what comes up. After all, we have a whole new year ahead of us. Anything could happen."

"We're going to have so much fun!" Jenna said. "This will be the best year ever. Don't you think?"

Peter smiled and put an arm around her shoulders. "Absolutely. Seniors rule!"

About the Author

Laura Peyton Roberts is the author of numerous books for young readers, including all the titles in the Clearwater Crossing series. She holds degrees in both English and geology from San Diego State University. A native Californian, Laura lives in San Diego with her husband and two dogs.